Heavenly Host
Unanswered Questions

Amanda Isaac

Published by

MELROSE BOOKS

An Imprint of Melrose Press Limited
St Thomas Place, Ely
Cambridgeshire
CB7 4GG, UK
www.melrosebooks.com

FIRST EDITION

Cover designed by Valerie Burton

ISBN 978 1 907732 51 5

Printed and bound in Great Britain by:
CPI Group (UK) Ltd, Croydon, CR0 4YY

FSC
www.fsc.org
MIX
Paper from
responsible sources
FSC® C013604

Acknowledgements

A big thank you to my wonderful husband Jim for showing patience through all my constant obsession with this piece of work, and the Writers Workshop for their guidance in putting me on the right path.

My beautiful children, Eloise, Sean & Simon for their wonderful love.

Extended love to my stepdaughter Tanya, her partner Ian and our first grandchild Kiera.

And a big warm thank you to Kelsey for having joint insight into the cover design.

Not forgetting my musical companions throughout this Journey, Muse (to whom I make reference twice in this book) and Kings of Leon, both of which got me back on track when I needed it most.

I salute you!

Writing a book! It's the best thing I've done in years.

Contents

Preface

Life is unpredictable, or is it?

Have you ever thought, when things take a turn for the worst, that perhaps there's something or someone guiding you through your decision, or maybe in another direction?

Book One

Introductions

1

Supportive Family

Well, that's me! Helena Garrett (Hels for short), twenty-one, long brown hair, which I tend to wear up most of the time as it gets on my nerves, always getting in the way, but for some reason I keep it long. Perhaps that has something to do with my dad commenting on it when I was a child; those memories have a way of sticking with you. And blue eyes, which I find strange, as I never inherited them from either of my parents. My friends call me an English rose, to describe my porcelain skin, which I have been very protective in keeping. I'm constantly told I've got my head in the clouds, maybe because people see me as a daydreamer. Well, they've mentioned it once or twice so I guess that's how they see me. However, I wouldn't describe myself as that, more free-spirited, with an open mind to life's unexpected. I live with my dad, Mike. He's the local town councillor in charge of growth and vibrancy. A pretty demanding job. We live in Teignmouth, a small seaside resort, in the middle of south-east Devon. Population a mere 19,687. A town small enough to forget it's here but big enough to attract gossip. We live on our own. My mum died three years ago, so it's still very raw for us. She was my best friend; we did everything together. And the emptiness she left behind for both of us was so huge. Every day for what seemed like a lifetime seemed to have no purpose to it at all. After her death my dad became more committed to his work, like it gave him a reason to live, and I guess it kept him from feeling so sad. I think about

3

her all the time. Memories everywhere I go. Everyone that knew her loved her instantly. I miss her so much! We were like the three musketeers, always planning stuff to do together. We were a real close-knit family unit.

With Dad so busy now, I end up spending a lot of time at home on my own, apart from when I'm at college. I attend the Art and Design College in Plymouth, a city at the bottom end of south-west Devon, on the border with Cornwall. Would-be students apply from all over England to gain a placement there, so I guess you could say it's a popular choice.

It's the end of my second year and the course has finally settled down. The classes were all a bit of a laugh at first; not sure about the direction the tutors were taking us all in but time has made it more structured. My mates are great! Rob and Jamie have been around since primary school days, so they know my family really well. They were a great support for both of us when Mum died. Always there when I needed them, offering help to Dad when he needed it. So I've never known a life without them in it. There are other people I've met since being in college but I never latched onto anyone else quite like the relationship I have with them. I sometimes think that maybe having girlfriends around, people I have something in common with, would be cool, so we could talk about things you just can't discuss with a guy, no matter how close you are. But on reflection, I'm not sure I would do that with them either. I tend to keep things pretty close to my chest, and as for the girlie stuff, I never did find it that interesting. As a child my mother would try to get me to stay in dresses and say how pretty I looked, hoping I'd get a feel for them, but it was a no-no. I never felt comfy in them, especially hanging around with the boys. So growing up with Rob and Jamie was really all I needed. I thought of them as my big brothers! Not because they are older than me but mainly because they had that protective element to them. They could be described as my very devoted extended family. But for all their devotion I reminded them they had their own lives, girl-friends and stuff. They didn't need to feel like they had to babysit me. I mean, I don't mind my own company; actually I quite like it, I guess. I'm like my mum for that. Many times she would take walks alone or spend time just sitting quietly staring out of the conservatory windows. I'd watch sometimes from a distance when she didn't know I was there and try to guess what she was thinking about. Sometimes judging from her expressions she seemed miles away. I often wonder where she was right at that moment.

Most nights I would fall asleep through a good film, with Dad sneaking in at the end of the night, to tuck in his little girl! When I was not at college, I'd be down at the local cinema. That's where I work part-time, two nights a week. Some nights Jamie and Rob will call in to catch up on the latest movie and usually we'll meet up afterwards for a burger in The Pantry, a local diner, down on South Street. It's become a local meet-up place for us. I don't know why, especially as I don't even eat any form of meat foods and they specialise in it, so I guess it's become habit. It's mid-August, nearing the end of the summer holidays. College will start again soon. September will be the start of my third and final year. The hardest yet, so I've heard. Preparation for our work to be exhibited in London later in the year: that is going to be a load of work in itself, and then, of course, a chance to travel, a gap year maybe before joining the throng of thousands of other hopefuls all looking for the same job. My brain has swollen from the thought of it, and it will come soon enough. Until then it's head down and earn the bucks before stressing about assignments.

2

No Preparation

It was midweek and I was due into work. Firstly I was meeting up with the boys down at the diner, so there was a need to hurry up and get sorted.

"Dad! You finished in the bathroom yet?" I shouted up the stairs. "I need to get in there."

"Yep! I'll be done in a minute," I heard him shout down.

The house we share is a little run down. It could do with a makeover but Dad doesn't seem to want to change anything when I mention it. I guess he just isn't quite ready to let go yet.

"Dad, come on! I need to get in there. I've got to get to work tonight you know."

"OK, OK! I'm on my way," I heard as the steam escaped from the open bathroom doorway.

Running for the number 86 bus from Exeter Road into town sent shivers up my exposed arms. It seemed to be getting colder. Strangely enough though the weather was really still quite nice. I don't know, maybe it was me just feeling colder. I get cold really easily but not all of the time. It was weird; I haven't always felt this way. I guess it started a few years ago. That made me think. A few years ago, which was around the time Mum died. Could that really be right? The thought faded as I clambered onto the now-arrived transport. At first glance the dimly lit bus looked pretty crowded. Making my way through the throng of hustlers, I took my place in the only position left, standing. The ever-patient waiting queue. Till someone hovers over the bell at the end of their destination, and then it's a free-for-all to jump into their seat. And then the pretending that you don't care about the overwhelming feeling of everyone staring and wishing to stab a thousand knives in your back, just because you made a selfish move.

Rob was already at the diner when I arrived.

"Hi, babes, how's it going?" he said across the room as he hurtled towards me for a peck on the cheek.

"Yeah! I'm OK. You?" I said. "How long you been here?"

"Not long," he murmured against my cheek.

"Where's Jamie?" I checked.

"Not able to make it; had to work," Rob informed me as we made our way to his chosen table. "I can't stay long. I'm meeting Becky later," he muttered low enough to sound disappointed for me.

Becky was his long-term girlfriend. They grew up together through primary school. They were well suited, had the same quirky interests. For a long time I think Rob's mother thought we'd end up together as more than friends. Often the innocent inhibitions would come out if we met up at his house but I never saw him or Jamie in that way. They were my mates! We stayed long enough to have a hot drink and a quick catch-up before leaving to start my shift.

It had been quite a busy time of late. A big sequel film was in full bloom; hence the place was packed constantly. My job was to show customers to their seats, so it could get a little heavy on the feet. But I like it; there's no hassle, no overbearing supervisor person pushing their personal status goals onto you. I'm thankful for small mercies!

Saturday I'd planned to go into Plymouth city centre to get what books I would need to return to college. I really hated shopping with a vengeance. I think my folks had passed that gene down to me. And I hated planning anything with anyone; it worked better when an idea would come into my head and away I'd go. No preparation! It's more productive!

3

Fear

Dad had offered to take me down; escort me really. Since Mum
wasn't around, he seemed like he was always trying to be two
people; making up for my loss, I guess, and his too. But I had
persuaded him I was going with Rob, Jamie and their girlfriends.
That wasn't the case, of course, but I think he bought the excuse
I gave him. As much as I loved my extended family members,
this trip had to be right for me to even tolerate. It had to be swift
and productive. Something I know would not have happened if
they'd tagged along! Not that I'm saying I wouldn't have enjoyed
their company, had fun and all that, but that was just it – nothing
productive would have been achieved. No! I had to go it alone. It
was no hardship anyway. I liked my own company. It was not like
I hadn't had much experience in that department.

I decided to take the train. The buses took forever, far too
long to get anywhere. It was about a forty-minute journey from
Teignmouth, so just time enough to get psyched up into the appropriate state of mind for a trip like this. I don't know why these trips
had become a chore. They never used to be; in fact I remember
really looking forward to any shopping trip Mum would suggest.
I guess that was just it – Mum's company was missing.

I connected my iPod to my ear and let the latest selection of
downloaded tunes take their effect. The train was empty but I still
had a bit of a scurry around before I made my final decision on
a seat. It's funny that. You have all the room in the world, the

best choice possible, but it still takes you a lifetime, so it seems, to make a decision over the most mundane of things. Too much choice can be a really dangerous thing!

The day was actually enjoyable, considering how much I hated all of this. And I even surprised myself by getting extras besides the books. The day was a winner! I'm not sure it would have been quite so, if I'd asked the gang along to join me in my little adventure.

The station was busy now: weekend commuters, happy shoppers, student types, excited couples with expressions of fun and expectation all over their faces, no doubt thinking of how their evening would pan out. It was pretty dark by the time I'd reached my connection. Most of the passengers had filtered off the train long before. I made my way across the bridge to the other side of the station to pick up the connecting train, which by my recollection was due in the next ten minutes.

The station was deserted. The newsagent stall was finished for the day. The ticket office was closed for the weekend. The modern machine equivalent was in the corner, taking over that non-personal task. Considering it was nearing the end of July, I was pretty cold. I was shivering. In fact, I tried to put my arms around myself to get some warmth over the outside of my bare arms. The goose bumps on my legs were starting to prickle up as I quickly stretched out my arms to give them a rub. I could hear the echo of trains from the tunnel as they crossed over adjoining lines, and I wondered if the one I was waiting for was on its way.

There was a clatter of noise behind me, distant for the moment but with indications of getting closer. I couldn't quite make out what it was as I turned to take a look over my shoulder. I reduced the noise in my ear by removing the remaining earpiece. The noise was rowdy, loud and getting increasingly closer. My first impressions made me uncomfortable, nervous even. The noise was close enough now for me to discern individual volumes. Some were louder than others, indicating the speakers' dominance in the group. I hadn't had a proper look yet, peering around the corner of the wall, my eager eyes watching desperately to catch a glimpse of the people who were now obviously making their way in this direction. The uncertainty about their appearance made me anxious and edgy.

I decided to get up and move along the platform from where I was sitting. I'm not sure why I did that. It wasn't as if there was anywhere else I could go; there's only so many places to hide in a station. I grabbed my stuff, pushing my hands through the handles on the bags. They were cold to touch as they brushed against the skin on my arms. At this point I wasn't sure what I was feeling. I ambled along the platform, back and forth, impatient to see what was coming to greet me from around the corner of the wall. The banter was loud now; the toing and froing of conversation implied there were a few in the group. I sank a little in my posture, my head automatically lowering into a defensive mode, as I spied the clattering throng making its appearance onto the platform. At first they were too busy, trying to get one up on the other in the conversation they were enthralled in. I carried on pacing, trying not to make any unnecessary distractive movements.

"If only this train would get here already," I was muttering to myself.

Surely ten minutes had gone by. In my irritation, I took a glance at my wristwatch, not noticing the figure now moving in my direction.

"Hey there, little darling," a voice whispered in my hair, as I pulled my head up. The smell of stale alcohol permeated through my hair, finding its way to my nostrils, as I found one of the guys nestling on my shoulder. The smell made my stomach churn, like heavy rocks tumbling around, mesmerising me to stand still. My hands were frozen at my sides with instant reaction to the sound and smell. My fingers fumbled with the object in my left hand, playing with the buttons whilst it irritably rested in my hand. I wanted to pull this object up to my face and punch in the relevant numbers, so I could make this vision come to an end. But my heart was beating so hard and fast, I thought it was going to drop out right there in front of me. I felt my breath shorten, and I rapidly became breathless. I was hyperventilating. I was stuck in this vision of hell or what I sensed was about to be hell. It seemed like I was there forever, but perhaps it was only seconds. I plucked up courage to pull away sharply, leaving the guy a little disorientated. Others departed from the group to join their mate at my side. The courage didn't last for long. They closed in around me, making it so difficult to breath. I tried to give myself some advice, to slow down, get a grip; how bad could this be? I wanted to speak, to shout out how I felt, my distaste at the way they were looking at me, teasing me.

Come on, get a grip, woman, I could hear my subconscious screaming at me. I could feel my chest rise and fall at a rapid rate as they all huddled round their mate, who was now toying with me. Irritating me. My eyes darted from one to the other, not really focusing on either one of them properly. I took a few steps backwards, feeling trapped. It was inevitable that they followed.

"Hey, little darling, where you going?"

"You're gorgeous." The original guy reached out and touched my shoulder.

I pulled away from his touch, like he had electrocuted me. The shock must have spurred me into action. I turned on my heels and moved away from the group. I didn't look back as I walked briskly along the platform but I didn't run. I wanted to but I didn't. I was still quite rigid in my stance, arms still frozen to my sides, thumbs twiddling with the buttons on my cell. I strained to listen for the onslaught of forward footsteps behind me, trying to equal my pace. I could feel the irritation of the bags I was carrying on my forearm, banging around against my leg as I rushed to pull my cell closer for a look, thumbs and eyes all the while trying to make sense of what I was trying so desperately to control, trying to dial the right number in my confusion of multitasking. I had switched off to what was going on behind me. I sensed the quiet around me but hadn't thought to even take a look at why.

"I've found it, my dad's number," I exclaimed as I thumbed through my contacts. I made the connection with my thumb as I automatically turned on my heels towards the group, as if to say "Ah! ah! Look, my dad's here now; he'll sort you out." However, the scene in front of me wasn't what I'd expected. They were gone. There was nothing! Not a single soul in front of me. I was aware that I was holding my cell out in front of me towards what should have been my nightmare scene, as if to frighten them. I looked around very cautiously, thinking that I had turned too far around on my heels, missing the group altogether, tricking myself. But no, there was nothing.

I was aware there was a slight buzzing in my ears. Not loud at all, just a very slight noise in the background. It was like the sound before your ears pop, when you're up on high ground. There were no other sounds, no movements of any kind, like watching a frozen state from a slow motion clip in a movie, except I was in it. My breathing slowed to a normal pace as I looked ahead. Something caught my eye from the shadows in the tunnel of the railway line. I could only describe it as a flutter really; nothing solid, I thought. However, I couldn't be sure. After all I was somehow in this dream state, so how could I be sure of anything? My hand, still with my cell in it, hadn't retracted back to my side yet. It was still hanging out there in front of me. My conscious mind was drawn to the faint chattering coming from it.

Oh! I'd forgotten – Dad!

"Uh, Dad! Sorry," I said as I flung my phone to my ear.

"Hels, what's going on? Are you OK? Is there something wrong?" I wasn't sure just how much commotion he'd heard, if any.

"I'm fine, Dad; everything's OK, I just got…" My attention was drawn to the railway line again. It was dark down there but there was something, something I couldn't quite make out. Was that an object I could see? It was so dark down there, shadows probably, but could that be eyes shining?

"Helena, are you there? What's going on, baby? Look, where are you? I'll come get you, OK?" he said. I guess he was troubled by my weird reaction. With my phone still fixed to my ear, I stretched myself towards the sight I was searching for in the tunnel.

"OK, Dad, that would be great." I could hear myself acknowledge the request but couldn't quite focus on the here and now. The feeling of the bubble-like state, the group's disappearance, with no sound and the images in the dark, was still etched on my mind. Was this a figment of my imagination or did something just happen that I was unable to explain?

4

First Sight

The journey home was reduced to yes and no answers, as I was still perturbed by my experience. The vision of the eyes in the darkness came flooding back, lodging in my memory, as I looked for other explanations. Had it been a figment of my imagination? Had there been something there in the darkness? And the group, where had they gone? The bubble feeling, had there been a reason for all of that? The memory made me uneasy, mainly because I couldn't provide myself with any answers.

As weeks passed, the situation in the station more or less disappeared from memory. My time was taken up again by life's little routines. Rob had initially enquired about my trip but I thought better of it and spared him the details of my out-of-body experience, only acknowledging what a success the trip had been. I was pretty busy in those last few days; work was plentiful and I was glad for it. Time was running out. College was due to start again in the next couple of weeks. I was ready. Necessary equipment was purchased for the return and I'd managed to save quite a bit of money whilst working through the holidays. This was it, third and final year! I didn't really know how I felt about that; plans were not at the top of the list. I think in some sense, you're not able to focus outside the here and now, perhaps because you don't want to. I didn't even know whether I was happy or sad about the fact that college life was coming to an end. Nevertheless it was happening and I would deal with it when it came. The guys had planned to meet up with me one night, after I finished work. It had been manic for months, thanks to the long-awaited latest premiere film. That night was no different. Once again my feet were really hurting me, as they had been most shifts.

This was the last of the extra shifts I was covering; college was back in two days. I managed to get all the stuff needed to start back and my mind was set to start swotting again. I was ready! I met the guys as arranged in the diner. They were in high spirits. They too had cut down their hours of work to compensate for college commitments. And like me, they were all geared up for the start.

The first week back was a little all over the place, as I tried to make sense of the new timetable, tutors and the geography of the classrooms, for that matter. It's surprising how everything looks so different after a summer period of rest. But that didn't last for long; routine soon embedded in and it wasn't long before you were looking forward to the next break. Luckily enough, though, the first week went in a blur. Time was spent mainly on my own at home for those first few weeks. The boys were too busy with their girls to hang out with me. No assignments had been set and of course I'd cut down my working hours to compensate for the heavy workload when it started. So now I was wishing that I hadn't been quite so hasty in turning down the extra shifts. I tried to put on my all-so-happy exterior but I think Dad saw right through me. I know he knew I was frustrated with the empty time. I met up with the guys when they weren't with their girlfriends but sometimes I felt I was taking up their time when really they wanted to be with them. A true gooseberry!

One night, my plans were to go to the pictures. Dad had a meeting, so he was going to be out most of the night. The guys were busy with other stuff. So it was a one-woman show tonight. It was an inexpensive social event for me anyway. That was a perk of the job. A couple of good films were showing that I was keen to see, and of course the big blockbuster was well into its cycle and packed all the time. One of the perks was that staff would also get the chance to see the first showing of any film, but the latest blockbuster had been pretty manic ever since it arrived, so there were very few of us who got the chance to see it. I was keen to see it but waiting for the hysteria to calm down was a better option.

I called into the diner on my way home. As I had predicted, the blockbuster film was packed. I was glad I'd decided against it. There weren't that many people in the diner when I arrived. A couple in the corner were huddled up, looking mesmerised with each other. There was an air of new love about them. I noted a few other people scattered around the room but my interest in them was very short-lived. I liked the way the diner looked when you first walked in; the ambiance of the place seemed so warm and cosy in the autumn evening. The evenings were clearly drawing in, so the tilly lights were lit, which gave it that glow effect.

"Hi, Helena, how's it going? You on your own tonight?" said the guy making his way to serve me at the counter.

"Yeah, I'm fine, Ben, thanks. I thought I'd call in on my way home," I said.

I had known Ben from secondary school and then sixth form. He hadn't followed up with college or uni like most of us did. He wanted to take some time out to, as he called it, re-evaluate himself. He was determined not to let others dictate his future. He was going to do something special with his life, make a real difference. He had very strong views on further education, think-ing that to take this direction was choosing the easy option in life. For the last few years, though, I didn't remember him setting the world alight. And as time went on, he never brought the subject up again for discussion.

"Home from where? Same as usual?" he asked as he grabbed a mug from the shelf.

"Yep, please. Cinema! I just treated myself to a movie," I replied as I scratched around in my pocket for some change to pay.

"Oh! Did you see *The Secret Heaven* then? Any good?" Ben asked as he buzzed around.

"No, no, I didn't get to see that; it's manic in there for that one. No, I saw *Baby Come Back*," I said as I laid the coins on the counter.

"Yeah! I heard it was busy in there, not that we've noticed an increase of customers in here," he said as he passed me the drink.

I found a really comfy armchair over in the back of the room. It was chilly but I was reluctant to start putting on my winter woollies just yet. It was my defiance of the end of the summer. But my body was clearly in revolt at that decision. I grabbed a book off the nearby shelf that I'd spied many times before. The lights weren't particularly good for reading here, so my eyes strained to make sense of the wording on the first few pages. There was no chance of getting the story from the cover; it was too dark to make anything out.

"Would you like a lamp brought over?" I heard this voice say in front of me. I was intrigued by how it sounded. Bright and uplifting in a way, soothing and reassuring, interesting.

I glanced up sharply. I hadn't even heard anyone walk over here. I wasn't quite prepared for what was clearly now stood in front of me.

"Oh! Sorry, I didn't hear you there," I said as I stared at this figure who was now beaming the most fantastic smile ever. His face was light all on its own! You couldn't help but be encapsulated by it.

"Sorry, I didn't mean to startle you. I just wondered if you wanted some more light, for your book?" he said as he pointed to the object that was now laid wide open on my lap.

"Oh right, sorry. Um!"

Pull yourself together woman, I silently told myself.

"Yes, that would be really nice, thank you! I didn't realise how dark it's getting now," I addressed him, as he moved out of vision for the briefest of time, to return with extra light.

"Thanks, great," I said as he bent closer to the side of me to attach the lamp to the socket. It was strange really. Although I wasn't totally taking note of what he was doing, it did seem like blurred time, fast but graceful. I noted his wonderful smell, as he pulled his face towards me for acknowledgement. It was a strange smell, not powerful like aftershave or deodorant but just as enticing. Earthy, maybe? Did that make sense?

"Is that OK for you, Helena?" His smile was still radiant.

"Yes, thank you so much," I said. "Can I get you a drink of something? Do you work here?" I couldn't tell. I hadn't seen all of him, just his face. I was mindful that I was throwing a lot of questions at him all at once. There was no proper time to react to any of them. "Please, why don't you pull a chair around?" I said as I gestured to the other armchair opposite. I was surprised at myself; I'd never done this impetuous stuff before. I placed the book on the table to my side as I made the gesture to stay. I wanted to get some change out of my pocket to get him a drink.

I stood but there was nothing. No voice, no being, no nothing. He had gone, disappeared like magic, and so had the smell. It was weird. I hadn't felt the change as he moved away. I never saw his face turn from mine. I was bewildered. I made a sudden burst forward to look frantically around for him. I could see nothing different to the layout that met me when I first came in. I quickly drank the remainder of my chocolate and made for the door. Maybe he had left. Did I say something to upset him?

It was really dark now. The streets were quiet. There was no sign of him out here either as I glanced around. It didn't make sense. As I my made my way home, still thinking about the situation, the image of his bright face was still etched on my mind. Where had he come from? But more importantly, where had he gone?

5

Chance Encounter

The next few days were merely a blur. My mind was tormented by the image of the face I had encountered. Such a sculptured face, silhouetted in the dark, shadowing light. Everything carried on much like before but I was missing; I wasn't myself. I hadn't been the same since my encounter with the stranger. I even asked Ben at the diner if he knew of him. He couldn't recognise him from my description. Mind you, that wasn't surprising. What sort of description could I give from the small amount of information I had? I retraced my steps of that night, visiting the diner at the same time, even sitting in the same place, hoping he would emerge from nowhere, much like he had before, but he didn't appear.

I had to push the cloud that hung over me to the back of my mind. I had an assignment that needed attention. I needed to prepare a paper on 'The Secrets of Generating Art Ideas', 1500 words on generating original ideas, design and composition. It shouldn't have been as difficult a task as I had made it; this was a relevantly easy first piece of work to accomplish. But I'd had some company of late, which put me back a bit in getting it finished. Dad had taken some time off from his busy schedule, and I was pleased to be the beneficiary. He hadn't planned to do anything but catch up with stuff around the house. Nevertheless, I was grateful for his presence.

Dad was a simple man. He had remained single. He had received one woman's advances about a year ago. They were great friends anyway. In fact, Kate had been one of Mum's closest friends. Sometimes she'd join us on one of our family adventures. After Mum passed, Kate was a great comfort to both of us, being there when I got home from school, making meals for us, generally just keeping life together for us, for when we wanted to re-enter it. Dad fell apart with Mum's departure. The routine of life afterwards for us was frozen, empty, just like the house. But Kate persevered, just by being there to paper over the cracks once we were ready to pick up the pieces of our lives. So it wasn't so terrible when Dad told me that Kate had spoken to him of her thoughts about opening up their friendly relationship into something more. Kate understood the reasoning behind Dad's decision not to take their relationship to the next level, and so their friendship remained, but I guess Kate's sudden infrequent visits after that didn't come as a surprise to both of us. Dad never made a big thing of it; he was just so grateful to her for the time she had given us when we most needed it. In a strange way though, I missed it. I don't mean I missed Kate herself as such, more that I guess I missed a woman's presence in the house. Mum had been such a figure for us, a tower of strength, of feasibility in our home life and all that was good in it. I knew that had gone now and maybe no one could bring that security blanket back, but the reality was that something had definitely brought that feeling back, if only for a short while.

"Hels, I'm going up to north Devon in the morning. Do you want to come?" Dad shouted up to me.

I had made a conscious effort of really concentrating on this assignment. I just needed to finish it!

"Hels, you up there?" Dad shouted again.

"Yeah, Dad! Sorry, I was studying. Did you say something?" I shouted down, as I detached myself from the numerous books scattered on the bed and made my way from the bedroom to the top of the staircase. Dad was waiting for my response as he stood at the foot of the stairs.

"Yes! I'm going to Lynmouth tomorrow and want to know if you want to come along." He put his foot on the bottom step to rest as he waited for my answer.

"Uh, yeah, OK! What time you going?" I started down the stairs.

"I want to be leaving around nine. I'm meeting up with Eric. Will you be OK, while I do that?" He followed me into the kitchen.

"Yeah, uh, I guess so." I was thinking now, planning in my head.

We set off as agreed at nine. The sky looked pretty good outside, so it looked like we'd get a dry day at least. Whilst Dad was with Eric as arranged, I'd decided to visit the information centre in the town to read about the flooding in the area years ago. Dad would contact me later, once he'd finished. We'd planned to have a day here. Ordinarily that would be a nightmare for me, given I hated this sort of thing, but on the whole I was feeling quite relaxed about it. Jamie had mentioned the place some time ago. He gone there with his mum and thought it was cool. We planned it as a venture when we were up this way next. How real was that! After taking in all the information about the horrific tragedy that had blighted his quaint town I made a tour of the harbour. The area was picturesque, with its expensive yachts, and dinghies that looked just as grossly expensive as the yachts. Jamie was right; it was a cool place. The weather really did the area justice, and it was really being kind today. It hadn't been this warm in a long while; in fact I had pondered over whether or not to finally give in to my body's reaction to the recent cold snap of late. But today's weather just reinforced my reluctance to put away my skimpy wear for hibernation. Dad was obviously enjoying his boy's time. I hadn't heard a peep from him, and lunchtime had come and gone.

I wanted to walk up to the top of the town, to where the castle was, to see down to the town, which was probably a good forty minutes walk. I sent Dad a text about my intention to go. I didn't want him ringing me saying he was ready when I'd only got halfway up there. His return text indicated that he and Eric were having a great time.

The walk to the castle was hilly. It sat on the top of a mound, surrounded by a man-made wall that enclosed it and continued all the way down into town. There were scattered benches on the way up to ease the hardship of the trek. I had to agree they were needed, but it was breathtaking. There were only a handful of people heading in this direction, clicking away with their cameras at the views below. The view was incredible! It was worth every step to get here.

I could feel the temperature drop quite considerably as I entered the building. The fragrance that hit me as I entered gave me a sense of being in a church environment – frankincense, myrrh. Beautiful but surreal! The floors were made of white marble, with a crest etched in the centre. It was magnificent! The building was very old, created in the 1600s. With its high ceilings and the paintings that hung from them, it seemed to smother my very being, as I looked up to marvel in its excellence. This was awe-inspiring; there was no doubt in that!

There were corridors that led off to other rooms with spectacular views but they all led back here. This room depicted wondrous beauty and passion. I visualised that this building and this room in particular must have been the centre of attention, where great ladies and gentlemen of real importance over the years walked and glided through in their finery. I took the winding stairwell off to the side of me, which eventually led up and out on to the top of the building. I could see for miles, and notice the existence of the vast grounds in which this building lay. Geez! It was blowy up here but quiet really. It was strange; I could see the flag at the top of the pole, blowing from the impact of the wind but there was no noise. It was deathly quiet. There was hardly anyone that had ventured this far up, just a few brave souls. I guess the steep steps had put them off. I peered through the wire meshing around the castle walls at the view below. The holes in the mesh were big enough for me to get a photo shot taken with my phone. It wasn't the easiest of positions, trying to keep it from shaking in my hand. The winds were really strong up here but the views were truly awesome.

"Hello again," a shrill voice sounded in my ear. I was still too focused on the image from my cell to catch sight of anyone sneaking up on me. I dropped my arms to turn around in the direction of the voice. There wasn't anyone around that I could see. I seemed to be up here alone now.

"Hello, Helena," the voice sung out again in my ear. I turned to try to face the voice, taking a position at the mesh surroundings to allow a view of the grounds below. A figure stood there in the middle of the grounds, looking up in my direction. It was difficult to see any details; the distance was too great. Nevertheless, I strained to make out anything from the shape. I wasn't even sure if the figure was looking up at me. But with only me here, who else could they possibly be looking at? However, who was it that was talking to me? There was no one around. Even if that person down there was looking up at me, I certainly wouldn't be able to hear anything up here; it was too far.

"Helena!"

I turned around sharply.

"Hello." A person spoke from over in the corner. As I looked, I was stunned by the resemblance to the figure I'd just seen below in the gardens. I quickly took another look through the mesh before returning to look at the man now sat in the corner. My puzzled expression must have been obvious. I was bemused that the man standing at the bottom of the gardens seemed very similar to the one now sat in front of me. The man wasn't looking at me though; he was staring at the floor. He was dressed in a dark suit, blue I think. It was difficult to really see. There was this aura of bright light that surrounded him.

"Hello, were you speaking to me?" I knew it was a silly question to ask him. How could it be him? Where did he come from? Wasn't he the guy that I saw in the grounds? It was all a bit weird!

"Yes, I did. Do you not remember me?" He peeled himself up from staring at the floor, displaying his stature to me now. His face was radiant, almost like a shinning star. The light seemed to have focused itself all around him. I'm sure that wasn't the case; it was probably my own perception. Otherwise that just would be too weird. I tried to get some focus on his features but the light was too bright. My body wanted to move forward, so I could feel a part of this conversation, but my instinct was to stay back, be cautious. I didn't know this man!

"No! I'm sorry, should I?" I tried to think this through. Had I met this man before? I was sure I hadn't. Anyway, I wasn't local to these parts, so there was no chance of anyone knowing me here. "I think you made a mistake." I sort of believed that statement, but then how could he know who I was?

"Do you not remember me? We met in your home town, in the diner a couple of months ago. You were sat in the dark with your book," he said.

Realisation kicked in. Thoughts rushed through my mind: No, this can't be… I thought I'd never… where did you go?

"You left. Where did you go?" I heard myself question him as I took a few steps closer.

The light around him seemed to dim.

"It's a long story. Unfortunately I had to leave. Did you enjoy your book?" He was now standing up. He didn't move at all. In fact I couldn't recall actually seeing him physically stand.

"Um, no!" I was confused. Him here. Now. Why?

"You did not like the book?" he asked with a puzzled look.

"Uh, no, sorry. I wasn't really reading that book; I just picked it up at the time you came. I'd seen it there before and was just curious, that's all."

"Before?" He looked puzzled.

"It's our local. We meet… I mean my friends and I meet regularly there. That's how I noticed the book there before." I hoped I'd explained myself clearly enough.

"Oh! I see," he said. "And why are you here today?" he continued.

"Ah well, Mike, that's my dad, is meeting up with an old friend in town and I thought I'd tag along. I'm not really into the shopping stuff, so I thought I'd come up here. It was something I meant to do if I ventured over this way. And today seemed like a very good opportunity. So here I am!"

I took a few steps closer. I was feeling surprisingly at ease, considering that I really didn't know this person.

"And you, why are you here?" I asked, gesturing at him.

I was very close to him by now. His stature was really breathtaking and his face had this magnificence that you just couldn't help but be mesmerised by. I hoped I didn't give anything away to him at this stage, but I was intrigued by this guy and wanted to know more about him.

"Well, I was sort of needed here." He walked towards me.

"Oh, really. Were you meeting someone?" I was curious.

"Yes, you could say that but my business here has finished now." He gestured with his hand at the stairwell.

"Oh! Right, well, I'm heading into town now; perhaps you'd like to join me for a drink?" I was hoping he would agree. I had no idea that I would be bumping into him here but now that I had, I wasn't ready to say goodbye just yet.

"I'm afraid I can't join you for refreshments but I'll escort you for some of your journey, if that would be acceptable to you," he said as he gestured to the corridor that led through to the main hall. I brushed past his arm and was overpowered by that smell of his. It had warmth that drew you in closer. It was definitely an attractive asset.

"Ladies first," he said.

I couldn't help but take in the amount of features in this magnificent room once again. I'm sure my previous thoughts had to have had some truth to them. I could visualise the people waltzing around in their finery. He walked with me down through the spiralling hill, talking all the while. Well, actually I was doing all the talking; he was just nodding in agreement in all the right places.

"Well, this is where I need to take my leave. Perhaps we'll meet up again. It was really good to see you again, Helena," he said as he stood still to emphasise his intention of changing course.

"Oh! Right." I was enjoying the company.

"See you again, Helena. Be safe," he said as he walked away.

"Yeah, sure, see ya." I wasn't totally thinking about what I was saying. I carried on down the hill as I looked back in his direction several times, watching him gradually disappear. My mind suddenly kicked in, and I ran a few steps back up the hill to catch his attention.

"Hey, wait up, you." I strained to see him. "Wait up. What's your name?" I had been talking to this guy all this time, met up with him twice, and still didn't know his name. How is that possible? But I wasn't going to find out today. He was gone; there was no sign of him. Disappeared, again!

Once again frustration was at its height. I felt cheated again. I just couldn't believe my luck. How on earth could I possibly end up meeting him, whoever 'him' was, in a place I never would have expected to? What were the odds on that!

I didn't mention to my dad my chance meeting with this guy. I hadn't mentioned it before, and so it was of no importance to him now. Dad seemed to have had a great time with Eric and it clearly showed on his face. It was great to see so much enthusiasm in Dad's face. I hadn't seen that in a long while.

Dad had the remaining nine days off. He set himself a few handy man jobs around the house, whilst I continued to concentrate on my assignment each night. The weekends came around pretty quick but as they came they were gone again. They were mainly taken up by working. I'd catch up with the guys down at the diner once in a while after shifts but I think my enthusiasm for meeting up there was down to the hope that there was a slim chance that he'd walk in. I hadn't spoken of him to Rob and Jamie. In fact, I hadn't spoken of him to anyone. I didn't do it consciously; it just happened. But then what could I possibly say? When they ultimately asked me questions, the answers would inevitably sound strange. So I didn't go there!

Christmas break wasn't far off; just over a week or so away. Rob and Jamie wouldn't be around much in the break. They usually spent the festive season with their other parent. Home was pretty quiet around the holidays. Dad did his best to make things festive. I think he felt he needed to make up for Mum's absence. Trimming the tree was aways a difficult task, one that was kept for Mum and I to do, and Dad tried his best to keep the spirit of it going. I appreciated it. I know it must have been difficult for him; all the emotions around that period could be overwhelming. As I was off from college for a few weeks I upped my shifts at the cinema. That was good for both of us. I tried to give Dad space to do his own thing, and myself things to do without Dad thinking he had to entertain me.

Things were quiet again at the picture house. The hype of the previous few months had died down. I was still popping into the diner from time to time but the guys weren't back yet. We still kept in touch most nights on Facebook. I kept them updated with my hectic schedule, or not, and they told me what they were up to. I think Rob found the whole stepparent thing more difficult than Jamie had. Rob lived with his father, so having to abide by another male's rules whilst he stayed there was difficult. But he kept it together for his mum's sake. He didn't see her enough to not make an effort. As for Jamie, it was his father who left the family home, so having a stepmum wasn't so bad. He seemed to get on with her kids and she was always mindful of the small amount of time Jamie had with his father, so encouraged their one-to-one time. And I think it helped that his mother and father still got on after their split. They were civil to each other!

6

Introductions

It would be a couple of days before my next shift. Dad was still off from work and knee deep in sorting out the house.

"Hels, do you want this old thing?" Dad shouted up from the cellar.

I had started spring-cleaning the kitchen. Thought I'd do my bit.

"Yeah, yeah, Dad, I'm here. What did ya say?" I shouted back, as I dropped the cleaning cloth in the sink and made for the top of the cellar door. Dad was now looking up at me with items in his hands.

"Baby, do you still want this?" He held them out.

"Hang on, Dad, I'll come down. I can't see it," I said as I made my way down. "Yeah, Dad, that's a shirt Mum bought me." I grabbed it from his hand. "But that can go," I added as I pointed to the other item. "What you doing, Dad?" I stared at the boxes Dad had dug out and was clearly going through.

"I thought it was about time I sorted this little lot out. And now is as good a time as any, don't you think?"

I nodded, not that I think he was waiting for my agreement anyway. "Dad, I can take them down to the clothes bank when you're finished, if you want. I'm going out later anyway, if that's…"

He cut me off. "Baby, that'll be great but I'm gonna be a while. Any good?" He was bagging up some bits.

"I'm not going till later this afternoon" That reminded me to go on up and finish the job I'd started. Time was moving on. "If you leave it up by the front door, I'll take it with me later."

I finished off in the kitchen and took off upstairs to get ready. I'd arranged to meet up with Billy. He was really Rob's mate from college. I'd met him a few times before, down at the diner. He tagged along in our little group. Tonight was really down to the guys. They'd mentioned I'd like a bit of company over the holiday period, being that they were away with their family. Again looking after me! Wish they hadn't though. I wasn't really bothered about going but thought better of it. A night out would be good anyway. I had no intention of staying too long. It really wasn't my scene but I said I would go and so I would.

Billy was having a house party. I'd been to one a couple of times before with the guys, so I knew how it would turn out. Starts off being conservative and ends up escalating into mayhem, with neighbours getting annoyed at the base booming from the speakers through the walls whilst they try to sleep. I decided on casual wear; however, that wasn't much of a decision, as I didn't possess anything else. I grabbed the bags at the front door that Dad had left. I could still hear him downstairs rummaging around.

"Dad, I'm off now. I've got the stuff," I shouted from the front doorway. I heard nothing. I dumped the bags down again. "Dad, did you hear me? I'm off," I repeated, whilst walking to the cellar doorway.

"OK, babe! I left the stuff by the door. Did you get it?" he shouted up.

"Yeah I got it, Dad. See ya later," I acknowledged.

"Hels, what time you home? Do you want me to come get ya?"

"Um, it's alright, Dad. I'm not gonna be late home anyway, so don't worry."

"Easy for you to say! Look, why don't you take the car? I'm not going anywhere tonight, so you might as well use it. And I'd feel better if you did and you'd be pleasing your old dad." He was now at my side, pushing the car keys into my hand, indicating I had no choice in this matter.

When I arrived at Billy's, the party was in full swing but it was still at the conservative stage. There was one problem about this party – no Jamie and Rob. Don't get me wrong. The party was good and Billy was a nice guy but I didn't really know anyone else. I'd sort of met a few of them before but didn't know them to have a conversation with and Billy – well, he was more the boys' mate. I wished they'd been here. I wouldn't have felt such a billy-no-mates. I stuck around for a while, pretending to be a part of the scene, but really I felt completely the opposite. It was still early when I made my excuses and left the party.

I'd made the decision to call in to the diner on the way home. I gave Dad a quick call to let him know. It would save him worrying, although when I called he was still knee deep in stuff downstairs, so I think his mind was preoccupied. The diner was semi-full when I got there but I managed to get a seat tucked away in the back of the room. My cell indicated I'd received a text. Jamie and Rob informed me they would be back the day after tomorrow. That was great news; I'd really missed them. I noticed the great smell as I wandered further back in the room. It wasn't of food or drink though. It was very familiar but I couldn't remember why. I grabbed the newspaper from the table. I hadn't seen much of the news of late, so it was a good catch-up.

"Hello again, Helena!"

I glanced up quickly from the article I was reading. "Hello!" I said but didn't really acknowledge who I was addressing, possibly because the brightness was so strong, obscuring my view of who was there. The smell seemed to intensify. I let the paper drop on the table and put my hand to my face to try and block out some of the bright light, but it still remained. I stood and the light was gone. He was stood in front of me!

"Hi, how are you? Really nice to see you again." He stood with both hands on the back of the facing chair.

I was shocked and pleased all in one moment. "Hiya." I was stunned to see him again and here of all places, on home turf! He certainly moved about a lot. "It's really great to see you again," I said as we stared at each other.

"Are you here on your own? Are you waiting for someone?" he asked.

"No, just me," I stated.

"May I join you then? Would that be OK?" He gestured to the seat he was leaning on.

"Yeah, of course. That would be great. I wanted to ask you a question anyway," I said as we both took our seats.

"What question would that be?" He gave a questioning glance.

"Well, what do I call you?" He continued to look questioningly at me.

"We've met several times and I still don't know your name," I answered him. "You see, you have me at a disadvantage." He threw another look. "You, somehow, have known my name from the very moment we met but I have no idea what yours is."

He gestured with his hand to indicate that he had gathered from my conversation what information I was after from him. I almost felt I was flirting with him. I hope I didn't make him feel uncomfortable.

"Yes, you're right." He looked thoughtfully at me. "I'm Gabriel, Gabriel King." He held out his hand for me to take.

I looked at it and flashed him a smile.

"Hello, Gabriel King. Very nice to meet you." I took his hand to shake and his smile widened. He returned the gesture.

"So, now we're properly introduced, what are you doing around here? Not that I'm not pleased to see you but we seem to be in a habit of bumping into each other, don't you think?"

He seemed to be really thinking about that presumption.

"Hmm. Well, there probably is a good reason for that, or maybe it could just be fate, you know." He looked questioningly at me again.

Now it was my turn to think about his comment.

"Do you believe in fate, Helena?"

It felt like he was really wanting me to think about his question. On a whole I guess I was open-minded to the idea of fate being the answer to some unexplained situations, but had fate taken a hand in me meeting Gabriel? I guess it was a possibility.

"Gabriel, I think I would need to give that some thought."

He smiled to acknowledge my reply and I mirrored him. It was so easy to do. I felt so at ease in his company. I'd had that feeling right from the beginning with him. Somehow he had this ability to draw you in, which made you feel that all you had to say was interesting. He wanted to know. It certainly was something I found I enjoyed being around. I thought about the numerous times we had met before today and how strange those times seemed to be to me, but maybe fate really had a hand in it after all. It certainly was open for debate at least.

7

Protector

The drive home had an air of excitement. Our meeting at the diner had gone far too quickly. I felt so at ease with Gabriel that I wanted it to last for a lot longer than it had but all good things had to come to an end. Gabriel had suggested meeting up again tomorrow, which I was more than happy to do. In fact I was hoping he would ask. I wasn't disappointed.

"Hels, that you? How did you get on?" Dad shouted as I came through the door.

"Yeah, Dad! I'm fine," I replied.

"How did you get on then?" he repeated, as I walked through to the lounge where he was slumped in front of the TV.

"It was OK. I didn't stay long, as you know." I didn't mention Gabriel. I wasn't sure what there was to say anyway. "I'm going up, Dad. I'm shattered," I said as I made my way to the staircase.

"OK, baby. You OK?" I heard as I climbed the staircase.

"Yeah, Dad, I'm fine. Just tired."

"OK! See you in morning. Love you," he shouted.

"Love you too!" I returned.

As I lay on my bed, the warmth from the shower I'd just had made me feel sleepy. My mind drifted, replaying the many topics both I and Gabriel had shared earlier. The more we spoke today, the more I felt we had so many things in common. The things we both enjoyed, and the things that I didn't like, which seemed to amuse him. As I replayed the scene in the diner back in my head,

35

I realised that actually I was the one that really had done all the talking, and he just listened with an interested look and a perfect smile when it was needed. His smile was something special. It said so much and it made me feel just fantastic. With that lasting thought in my head I drifted off to sleep.

My night's sleep was not particularly restful. I seemed to continually wake up, always with the same consistent thing on my mind. Gabriel. I couldn't pin point it down to any real reason but maybe it had something to do with meeting up with him again today. He definitely made an impression. The thought of seeing him again was so exciting, I felt a little foolish for thinking that way. I felt like it was a first date, whatever that felt like, but I guessed that I wasn't the only one to feel this way. I'm sure it was a natural feeling. But this was all new to me. I'd never done any of this before. The only males I spent time with were either the guys or my dad. But this felt a whole lot different. I shouldn't get ahead of myself though. We'd just met. We really didn't know each other; I shouldn't presume anything more than what it was, a chance to meet up with a new-found friend. And I was more than happy with that, for now anyway.

Dad left for work early the next day. He'd made plans to meet up with Eric, his mate in North Devon, again. He'd asked if I wanted to go along but I made my excuses, of course not telling him the real reason, that I had no interest in going with him.

I heard the faint ringtone of my cell. I quickly searched around to find where I'd last left it. I realised I was getting closer as the ringtone to one of my favourite band's music got louder. I found it and thumbed the touch screen to answer the call.

"Hi," I said.

There was no reply, just silence. I pulled the cell away from my ear to take note of the contact on the screen. I didn't recognise the number. I returned it to my ear.

"Hi, is anyone there?" I repeated.

"Yes, Hels, it's me. Gabriel," his husky voice replied.

"Gabriel?" I was shocked and a little confused to hear his voice.

"How did you know my number?" I was trying to think whether or not I had given it to him.

I couldn't remember I had!

"You gave it to me yesterday. Don't you remember?"

I didn't, I was sure of that, but something made me doubt myself. I don't know why.

"Uh, OK! Is something wrong then? Are we still meeting up?" I realised I sounded panicky and pathetic. Desperate – not a good look.

"Yes, don't worry. I'll be there!" I heard a little chuckle in his voice and I visualised a little smirk in his smile, as if he'd guessed my thoughts. Definitely not good.

"Everything's fine, nothing's changed." His voice was soft and reassuring, as my panic began to wane and a smile replaced it. He'd called me Hels. He'd never done that before. I had no intention of questioning it. I liked the way he said it. Too much!

"I just wanted to know if you wanted to meet up at your home. We could walk to the diner together, if you'd like?"

"Um, yeah, Why not!" I was still thinking about how he got in contact with me, convinced I hadn't given him my number.

"OK. I'll be there in a moment," he said, whilst my mind was still preoccupied.

"OK." The other end went silent, and I dropped the cell from my ear. Wait! I realised I hadn't told him my address. But he was gone. I kept my cell in my hand, anticipating the returned call from him.

The knock at the door disturbed my train of thought, pulling me away from my preoccupation. There was a second knock which spurred me into moving to answer it. I was somewhat shocked at what met me on the other side of the front door. Gabriel was stood there. But how? How did he know where to come and so quickly?

There was that smell again.

"Gabriel! How did you get here so quickly?" I said as I gestured to invite him in.

"It's not that far," he said.

"What, so you live nearby then?" This was my explanation for him getting here so soon. But the ultimate question on my mind was, how did he know where to come in the first place?

"But how did you know where to come?" I asked, as we stood together in the hallway. "'Cause I know I never told you," I added questioningly.

"Hmm." He stood with his hands in his pockets. I couldn't help noticing how great he looked today, dressed in another fabulous suit. "I heard your friend Jamie mention it."

To be honest, I was a little intrigued to know in what context Jamie had spoken about me and where I lived. I didn't even know Jamie knew Gabriel. It seemed strange. But anyway…

"Jamie. You know him?"

"No."

"But you said..?"

"I said Jamie mentioned it. I didn't say we knew each other." He was staring at my face. I guess he realised I was questioning a few things in my head.

"But, what does that mean? I don't understand?" I was confused.

"He was talking to his mate – Billy, is it? And, well, your whereabouts were mentioned. I happened to be there and, of course, when you and I met, I put it all together," he said, filling in the details.

"Oh! Right, I see." I was trying to plant the situation in my head. "I'll grab my stuff and we can go, OK?"

I whizzed around the house snatching what I needed before making for the door. It was still playing on my mind. It didn't seem to add up somehow.

"My car is outside. I thought maybe if you were up for it, we could go out for a drive. We can still go to the diner first if you want. I'm happy to do whatever you want."

"OK, yeah, that sounds great. We don't have to go to the diner. In fact, let's not. It would be cool to do something different anyway."

He was showing me to his car. Wow! Nice car, real classy. Not that I was into cars or anything but I could recognise a nice one when I saw it. You couldn't help but admire it.

"So, Miss Garrett, where would you like to go?" he said as he shot me one of his smiles. "I'm at your service, madam." The engine purred softly, like a cat enjoying its cuddle. He took a cocky bow, like he was my knight in shining armour. We laughed. I'm not sure what we were giggling at but it so fitted the situation perfectly.

As it was, our destination was a mystery. I left the decision to Gabriel. I was just happy to be in his company. We talked non-stop about all sorts. It was a different kind of conversation this time. Gabriel actually joined in. I guess he felt comfortable now with me. Sometimes the discussions we had were so engrossing that I hardly knew we were moving. And his driving was flawless. Light even. You could say it was almost flightlessness. I had no idea where we were going; the road seemed to wind up and around, in a never-ending spiralling motion. The views below were breathtaking. I could smell the foliage in the woodland that surrounded us and the refreshing scent of the sea in the distance. I asked him our destination but he just said, "You'll see. All in good time."

Actually it seemed exciting, like a little adventure.

"You know, you're a good driver, or perhaps it's just the way the car drives," I said, breaking off from staring at the view below.

"What does that mean?"

"Well, I can see we are moving very smoothly in this fab vehicle but I feel no motion from it. So it's hard to make out whether or not it's your driving or the suspension of the car."

I shifted my face from the passenger window to look at him. He didn't turn to meet my stare. He just smiled slightly.

"I'll take that as a compliment then." His smile widened.

"You're welcome!"

It wasn't too long before we made a stop. I guessed we'd reached our destination.

"OK. So we're here."

The engine died.

"Right, OK!" I grabbed my coat from the back seat where I flung it earlier. Not many cars here. In fact it was pretty empty.

"I thought if you were up for it, we could walk a while. It's a great walk. Are you up for it?" he asked.

"Yeah, that sounds good. I'm not such a great walker but I'll give it a go."

"Don't worry too much. It's not that kind of a walk. It's quite casual and there's a tea room a little ways in," he reassured me.

"OK! Well, if it gets too much, maybe you'll have to carry me the way back!" I was joking, giving him a sly smirk.

"I have no problem with that. I'm happy to carry you all the way there and back, if that's what you wanted." He had a real sincere look on his face. And I believed him!

"OK! OK! Gabriel, I'm not an invalid yet, you know. I said I would give it a go and I will," I chuckled. Talk about damsel-in-distress scenario, I thought to myself.

The walk was just as he said, leisurely and enjoyable. The woodland surrounding us was amazing, so much life breathing in its environment. We reached the tea room as he predicted in no time, which was a little disappointing only for the fact that it interrupted the zest of the conversation. The tea room had been a wooden log house in the middle of dense woodland. It was really quaint-looking.

Inside, the layout was dedicated to serving the public hot food and drinks. A little section was cornered off as a gift shop. There was an area that had a homely feeling, a place to relax near the glowing log fire. And this was the area we decided to sit in.

"Helena, are you OK? Warm enough?"

"Yeah, I'm good, thanks! I'm so glad for the fire though. I was getting really cold out there." I was rubbing my hands up and down my arms to get some warmth into them.

"Oh! Right. But what do you think of the walk though? Are you enjoying it?" he asked, looking a little awkward. Maybe he was thinking he should help in the process of warming me up.

"Yeah, it's great, a really nice place. And I'm managing to keep up with you, which I'm surprised at myself."

The warmth from the fire began to thaw my fingertips. As I watched the splinters of wood spat out a dance of flames and ended as glowing embers. The room was empty except for us. I guess that had something to do with the time of year.

"You know, Gabriel, I've managed to talk loads about me since first meeting you but I know very little about you. Like for instance, how you came to be in Teignmouth? How long have you lived around here? And how come we've never met before?" I was conscious I was staring at his hand as it sat on his stomach. I was taken in by its shimmer. There was a real noticeable glow to it, like glitter rubbed in. My gaze broke when he spoke.

"Helena?" He said to get my attention.

"Uh, oh yeah, sorry." I turned to his quizzical features.

"I'm not that interesting. I'd much rather hear about your

adventures. I find them fascinating. He won me over with a big, broad smile. Wow! That could have lit up the whole room! No matter how often you saw it, you could never get used to it.

"Uh, uh. You're not getting away with it that easy. I really want to know all there is to know about you." My face must have had a pleading expression.

"Honestly, Helena, I'm really not that interesting, as I told you. This area is where I was born but I've been away. I only returned a little while back."

"Really?" I was puzzled.

"Yes, my family have lived here for many, many years. The family home I live in now was left there empty in case I decided to return. They moved a few years ago. I went to live with my mother's family in Cornwall years ago when I was a small child, but decided to return to the house recently. Having no childhood here has given me no memories as such. So it's like starting my life over."

"So what made you come here?" I asked, interested in his reasons for coming back.

"I know it seems strange, to set up in a home you've had no history in. It makes no sense, but how can I explain? I was drawn here!" He had that distant look about him as he told me his story. "The day we met in the diner; you remember?" he prompted.

"Yes, of course." How could I not remember our unforgettable encounter? His face, that gorgeous smell, captivating me, making me his willing victim. How could I lose those overwhelming memories?

"Well, I was there when you came in. I didn't see you come in but – it's going to sound crazy – but I felt you there. Your presence." He looked at me with a sort of longing expression, waiting for my reaction.

"Oh! I see." I was still trying to get my head around his story. I leaned forward with my hands cupped in between my knees.

"See, I told you it sounded crazy!" he continued. He leaned forward, copying my posture.

"No! I don't think that at all. I mean, has this happened to you before, with oth—"

He interrupted me. "No! Just you. Since I got here, it was as though I was meant to meet you, be around you. Does that sound weird?" he explained, shaking his head, with a frustrated expression on his face.

I think he was looking for some signs in my facial expression giving away what I was really thinking.

"And the time we met up at the castle. No coincidence?" I asked.

"If I lied and said yes, would that make things seem any better?" He had that pleading look in his eyes. Eyes that said, please, I'm asking for some help here, please make it be normal, make me be normal!

Thinking about it, I actually felt really flattered, special somehow. How could that be weird?

"Gabriel?" I smiled at him. "Hey! Well, I count myself real lucky!" I hoped the smile I continued to direct at him would ease his turmoil, which was now etched on his face.

"Really! You sure? I even find it creepy myself. Maybe I should just move back to Cornwall. I never had these feelings there. It would be my only way of keeping away from you." His head was in his hands, as if he was fighting with his frustration.

I decoupled my hands and reached for his.

"Gabriel! Please don't. I mean, I'm flattered you feel you need to be close to me. To be my protector, bodyguard perhaps. Hey! Even my guardian angel." I smiled at him in order to get his attention. It worked. His returned smile was so radiant that I knew from that moment I was taken in.

8

History Lesson

We stayed for a while longer, talking as before. I was surprised at how quickly time passed whilst we'd been here, as I glanced at the overhead gift clock that depicted the shape of a sheep. It went in line with the rest of the theme here. There were so many more questions I wanted to ask but I thought better of it, for today at least.

For some reason the walk back to the car didn't seem so far. It's funny how it always seems to feel that way when you go travelling. The journey back has a feeling of somehow being shorter. It's a strange observation but I think expectation has a hand in there somewhere.

It wasn't long before we were outside my house again. The house seemed quiet. Dad was obviously not back yet. There was no sign of his car anywhere.

"Would you like to come in for a minute?"

"Yeah sure, OK." He looked like he hadn't expected me to ask, which was something of a novel response.

As predicted Dad was nowhere to be seen.

"Drink?" I offered as I quickly scanned the area for any embarrassing untidiness.

"No, thanks! I'm fine." He looked a little awkward. He was still stood in the doorway.

"Gabriel, have a seat. I'll be back in a minute. I need to use the, er, loo, you know?" I said as I edged towards the staircase. I noted butterflies in my stomach, and an air of nervousness that I hadn't felt before.

"Gabriel?" I said when I returned. He wasn't in the kitchen where I left him.

"Hels! I'm in here." His voice was coming from the lounge.

"You've got some really great family photographs here. Is this your dad?"

"Yeah, that's Mike! That was taken at one of his councillor dinner parties last year."

"And this one?" He was looking at a photograph of me and my mum.

"Oh, that's my mum! That's one of my favourites."

By now he was scanning all the photographs displayed on the wall. He seemed really engrossed in them. Mum had a real love for pictures. She said it made her feel like she belonged. History was being made for future family generations. Sometimes I would watch her admiring them and smile as she gently rubbed her hands over the frames.

"Your parents, are they due back soon?"

"Oh, I don't know when Dad will be back. Soon maybe."

He pulled away from the wall now and gave me a little smile. "And your mother? Where is she?"

We took a seat.

"Oh, she passed on three years ago."

He looked at me with a sudden sad expression. No different to what others had done when they heard the news. He also adopted that immediate silent treatment, not knowing what to say, feeling awkward, so deciding to say nothing.

"Oh! It's OK. I can talk about her now without getting upset. I just think about all the great things we did as a family unit. I value those memories very much. Of course I miss her like crazy, especially around the girlie stuff we shared. She was a great mum. We really were close!"

45

"And your father? How is he?"

"He's a lot better now. He was bad for a while; we both were, but we're there for each other, so we get through. We're really tight, always have been, which really helps at a time like this."

I talked loads about my family and how it was and how things are now. He seemed really interested about our past adventures and stuff. It was great talking about that stuff again. I hadn't done that for a long time without crying myself to sleep. He asked about my relationship with Rob and Jamie and seemed intrigued by the bond we all shared. On reflection, he also seemed a little sad, when I'd catch him in moments of what seemed like deep thought, whilst I went about stuff.

"Well, Hels, it's been really great. I think I should be making a move now, but before I go, I wonder if you would consider going for a meal with me tonight?"

Nervousness was taking a hold again. I wasn't expecting that.

"Your friends are back tomorrow, right? And chances are you'll be otherwise occupied, so I thought..."

How did he know that? There was no way he could know that but he did. But how? I wasn't about to go into that now, though. I'd get my chance at some point. It was really strange that he knew stuff like that.

"Yeah, I'd like that. Although I should warn you, I don't have anything special to wear, so I hope it's not somewhere classy."

"Helena, I'm sure anything you wear will be just fabulous. And anyway, to put your mind at ease, I thought if you didn't mind we could eat at my place? What do you think? OK with you?" He was already heading for the door.

"Wow, all in one day!" I said to myself as I followed him out to his car. He looked back with a wry look on his face.

"Hope it's not too much for you. I'm not being too forward?"

It was as though he'd heard me.

"No, it's fine. I'm looking forward to it," I replied. Although God knows how I'll be later on, I thought. My nerves were already doing overtime. Time to self-soothe!

I could hear the sound of gravel crunching under tyres as I spied Dad arriving home.

I introduced them to each other. "Dad, this is Gabriel."

"Gabriel," Dad said as he took his hand.

"Mike. Nice to meet you!"

"Yeah, you too." Dad's gaze was focused on Gabriel's face. "Do I know you? You look familiar!"

"No, probably not. I haven't been here in some years," Gabriel informed him.

"Oh, right. Well, perhaps you have a double. Hels, I'll see you in a minute," Dad said as we watched him disappear inside.

"OK. Well, I'll pick you up, say around seven-ish, OK?"

"Yeah, thanks. Seven. Great."

And he was gone.

The self-soothing hadn't gone to plan. Nervousness was at fever pitch now, as everything from the wardrobe was now in a heap on the floor. Nothing seemed to match. I really needed to do some shopping, but it wasn't one of my favourite pastimes.

Gabriel was on time. The nights were drawing in; it was starting to get dark early again. I never did really understand the whole changing the time thing through the year.

"How far to your place?"

"Not far now."

And true to his word, it wasn't.

The house was set in woodland surroundings. It stood alone. It wasn't any bigger or any smaller than any other house, but it looked old. As we entered it, I sensed a strange air about it. I stood for a moment looking at the brightly lit porch. It was a strange light, not like a bulb light but something else; a whiter light, much brighter.

"Helena, please come in." Gabriel extended his hand towards me.

"Yeah, of course, thanks."

The light seemed to follow us into the house but I don't remember Gabriel turning on or off any lights, and yet it was there and then not when we passed through each room, I noticed as I glanced back. Considering the house from the outside didn't seem any larger than any other, it sure felt bigger inside as we briefly passed through each area.

God! He smelt good. And he looked so cool! He removed his jacket and hung it on the back of a chair in the dining room. I looked around and noted that the cups, plates and stuff were all laid out on what looked like a very old dresser, and how everything looked in place, pristine, like they had never be used.

"Can I take yours?" Gabriel asked, pointing to my coat.

"Do you mind if I keep it on for a moment? I'm feeling really chilly."

"Oh! Is it cold in here? I don't really feel it any more. Guess I've got used to it. Hang on. I'll get the fire sorted. You take a seat over there and I'll be back in a minute."

And he was gone. I perched myself on the edge of an easy chair situated in the middle of the room, surrounded by other chairs and a sofa. These were old as well.

Gabriel was back. It was hard to imagine how he'd completed that task so quickly.

"All sorted. It won't be long. It'll soon warm up in here. Now! How about that drink?" he asked as he stood there with his hands in his trouser pockets, beaming that perfect smile at me.

He had that canny knack for always being right. It wasn't long before I was removing my coat and feeling comfortable enough to sit relaxed in the chair.

"Your drink!" he said as he handed it to me. "Dinner won't be long. I hope you like it. I don't cook for myself normally. It's never the same when it's only you that's eating. No appetite!" he continued as he was toing and froing from the kitchen.

Gabriel had really gone to town. Everything was laid out beautifully in the dining room. The furniture looked really old here too. It was antique, I think. In fact the whole house had that feeling of history about it. I guess that's why it felt so cold in here.

The meal was done to perfection and Gabriel, ever the gentleman, was a great host.

"Gabriel, that was really great. I've never had lobster before. Fab meal, thanks." I noticed he had hardly touched his food. "Are you not going to eat?"

"Oh no. Not hungry," he replied as he started to clear the plates from the table.

"Can I help?"

"No, it's OK, I'll sort it later. Shall we?" he said as he escorted me through the hallway.

The walls were covered in paintings; really old paintings, I think. Not that I was an expert, but didn't have to be to know that there was something special about them.

"Family?" I asked, pointing to a painting of a beautiful raven-haired woman and an elegantly dressed man. It wasn't a modern piece, rather one of those you were more likely to see in a classic book like *Pride and Prejudice.* I was aware of feeling instant curiosity about this painting, as though for some reason I had a closeness with it. There was something familiar that I just couldn't see.

"Yes, my mother and father."

"Are you close? I know you said you spent your childhood with your aunt but…"

"No, not really. My father visits me now and again."

"Oh, I see." I was aware how sad I sounded. "And what about your mother? Does she not see you?"

"I never knew her. Unfortunately my mother died when I was born." He turned to catch my gasp. I was never expecting that. "My father has never spoken of her but my aunt used to tell me a few things."

"Were you not curious to know about her? You must have missed her."

My own thoughts of my mother came flooding back. The times she would laugh and sing in the shower. I smiled at the memories that whizzed through my head.

"When I was younger I wanted to know but my father would only become angry at the mere mention of her name. So after a while it just became the norm not to ask. And as I wasn't around him much, I guess my aunt became my parent figure."

"Did you not want to know why he was so angry?"

"I thought about it once or twice but thought better of it. I asked my aunt once why he was that way but she told me that he found it very difficult without my mother. She said that they had been with each other forever. So I guessed that having that kind of bond then losing it would make anyone feel that way."

"And so what kind of relationship do you have now? Is it better?" I thought of my own relationship with my Dad and how strong it was. Needing each other, especially at the time of our loss. And how strange it must have been for Gabriel not having that bond. How does that make you feel?

"It's very polite between us!" he said.

I thought that he would undoubtedly show his feelings, frustration at least for what clearly sounded like a fragile relationship between father and son, yet there was nothing in his voice to indicate passion or anger.

"And so you live here all alone? Do you not get lonely?" I asked, changing the subject.

We made for the lounge area. The furniture matched the rest of the house, a gem for the historian. Worth a fortune, I shouldn't wonder.

"I used to think that there was no sense in me being here. I couldn't understand why I felt I needed to be back here. After all, it wasn't as if it was my home. But then it all made sense."

"What made sense?" I was intrigued.

"The day I first saw you! You were standing in the station at Plymouth waiting for your connection. Do you remember?" He was looking deep into my eyes now as we stood together.

I was desperately trying to remember when that was. My mind searched frantically for memories. And there it was. That time the previous year I had gone to do some shopping. It was the one thing I hated the most but I planned it on my own without the guys. I was waiting for the connecting train to take me home. And there were those guys, the phone call to Dad, and then they were gone. The eyes staring at me in the darkness. The tunnel. I couldn't see, it was so dark down there. I remembered the desperate feeling I had standing on that platform. Remembering it again brought it all back.

"You remembered." He must have guessed from the expression on my face.

"Yes I remember but we never met there... How do you know all this? What I mean is, how did you know me? There was no one else there." I'm sure I must have looked puzzled. I really was confused.

"Well, Hels, that's not strictly true." He was holding both my hands in his now.

"What do you mean?" I was totally flummoxed. I stared at my hands surrounded by his.

"Those guys at the station. Surrounding you. Smelling of alcohol and being a nuisance. Didn't it frighten you?"

Why did he ask a stupid question like that? Of course I was frightened. I was petrified! I hated this!

"Yes, of course. I thought they were going to…" I was aware of the warm, wet tears as they streamed down my face. I hated how this still made me feel. After all this time, that fear was still there. It had gone nowhere.

Gabriel pulled me to his chest as the tears flowed uncontrollably now. I could see the shimmer of his white skin glistening through the gap in his shirt, his head resting on top of mine, his hands still embraced around mine. But through my pain, I still couldn't understand how he could know so much.

"Gabriel." I pulled away from him. "How?" I wanted to know how he could know these things.

"What?"

"How is it you know all this stuff? I don't understand. Are you saying you were there? And if so, where? There was no one apart from me on the platform."

"And those guys!" he corrected me.

"Yes, and those guys. But you, I don't remember."

"I didn't say you saw me. I was there, watching."

"What?" I was curious. Watching? Why?

"I can't explain to you in any words that make sense why I was there. Because I don't know myself."

"What?" I was really puzzled now.

"Hels, what I mean is, I somehow needed to be there. I didn't know why. Logically I can't tell you why; it just felt right when I was, especially when I felt your fear." He looked a little troubled.

"Wait a minute. You said you could feel my fear?"

He removed his hands from mine and placed them in his trouser pockets, whilst his gaze dropped to the floor.

"What do you mean by that?" I was trying to get him to look up with my head bent towards his. He walked towards the back of the room, as if he wanted to put some distance between us. There was an obvious sense of that now.

"What's wrong? Have I said something?" I couldn't understand why he needed to walk away.

"I'm sorry, I shouldn't have said…" His face was still pointing downwards towards the floor. He looked so sad!

"Gabriel, please, what's wrong? I want to know."

It wasn't intentional, but I was crossing the room. I didn't like how the distance felt between us now. I wanted to get back the moment I had just had.

And there it was! As I reached for his forearms, he lifted his head. His face was still tinged with sadness. I smiled, hoping to break his discomfort. He slowly pulled his hands from his pockets. My grip around his forearms broke.

"Helena, I think we should be getting you back now. It's late!"

The moment had gone. The few minutes of closeness between us was now replaced by cold, detached, awkward conversation. I hated it! What had I done? There was clearly something upsetting him but what, I didn't know. I really didn't understand at all.

9

Gabriel

Gabriel was exceptionally quiet in the car on the way home. Not that he was a big talker anyway, but the situation in the house didn't help, although I still didn't know what that was all about. One minute he's telling me he was there at the station, the next he didn't want to talk about it. What was all that about? He would have been better off not bringing it up in the first place. Then we would not have this coldness between us now. It made no sense. I tried to make light of the lack of conversation between us but he didn't rise to the bait, clearly not being in the mood for it. It wasn't long before we were parked outside my front door. There were no lights visible from inside. I guessed Dad had gone to bed. I was glad really. I didn't want the third degree from him on the way in.

The engine died. The awkwardness between us was clearly visible but seemed heightened by the silence within the car.

"Helena?" Gabriel turned towards me with his hand slowly grabbing mine. His face wasn't stony as before. It was a lot more mellow now. I hadn't sensed it coming. There were no indications, but it was welcome.

"I'm so sorry about tonight. I never wanted to upset you."

Our faces were inches from each other. I could smell his scent as it engulfed the small confined space of the car. I still sensed his unhappiness. At what, I really wasn't sure.

"Wait! Look, Gabriel, you really have nothing to say sorry for. I've really enjoyed tonight. Haven't you?" I asked. I really didn't want to get back into all that stuff in the house again, ruining the moment. I wanted us to get back on track again.

He smiled. The radiance lit up the whole car.

"Yeah, sure have!" he answered.

I sensed an intensity between us. When he looked at me, it felt as though he was reading my soul. His hands hadn't moved, neither had his face. Both focussed on me. I felt nervous again, not sure what to do or say. So not a word was spoken. I guess it wasn't needed anyhow. I don't know how long we sat there. It didn't seem to matter to either of us anyway. Finally the intensity of the moment was broken by light strewn out across the bonnet of the car. We both looked. It was coming from the house. I was wrong. Dad was in after all, and no doubt an interrogation was on the cards when I got in.

"OK. Well, I suppose I'd better go in," I said as I reluctantly decoupled my hands from his and grabbed my bag. Although the feeling of nervousness made it painful to try and keep things together and not get carried away in the moment, I liked the excitement the butterfly feeling gave me in my stomach.

"Hels?" Gabriel got my attention again by grabbing hold of my forearm before I left the passenger seat. "See you soon, right?" he asked.

"Yeah, of course," I replied, probably sounding flippant as I got out of the car. I hope he didn't see it that way. I wanted to reassure him, and of course myself, that our meeting up again would happen sooner rather than later. "Gabriel! Soon, yes?"

His smile said as much.

As predicted Dad was in the kitchen, waiting to bombard me with questions about my evening. But I managed to get away with yes and no answers for now. I was sure the answers would need to be meatier next time to satisfy his curiosity.

My head was all over the place when I reached my room. I replayed from memory the conversations we had during the evening. Gabriel telling me about his family. The loss of his mother. Never knowing her. His relationship with his father, or lack of it. My trip to Plymouth. Him knowing all about my fear that day. Real crazy stuff! I played these thoughts over and over again in my head as I tried with difficulty to get an internet connection. The boys would be back tomorrow, and I feared all would be changed. I wanted to see Rob and Jamie. I'd missed them a lot! But there was Gabriel now, so where did he fit into all of this? Maybe he wouldn't want to. How would they take to him? They had no idea about Gabriel. I hadn't mentioned him or anything. I didn't know where to start, for that matter. I needed to tell them tomorrow. I don't know why I was getting so protective of him. Gabriel was just a friend. I was allowed more than them, I told myself. The boys would understand.

I met with Rob and Jamie in the diner as planned. It was fab to see them. I'd really missed them but I hadn't realised how much until they were back. We caught up with what they'd been up to, the time they'd spent with their families over the holiday period. And I gave my rendition of what had been going on for me. But of course I made my time sound as dull as theirs, making no mention of Gabriel. I would do that later at some stage. I needed more time.

Time passed quickly over the next few days; in fact it flew by. I'd worked a couple of extra shifts anyway, covering for one of the girls. I'd seen the guys a few times but they too were working extra hours before returning to college the next week. My assignment was completed. I was relieved. It took a little longer than anticipated but I got there eventually. It was my own fault, leaving everything to the last minute. Dad had long since returned to work, so I was back to my own company again. I hadn't seen Gabriel since our departure at the house a week before. No phone calls, no texts, no little surprise encounters. I thought about contacting him but surprisingly there was no return number from last week's phone call to my cell. All trace of the call had been removed somehow. When I had moments on my own, especially at night when it was so quiet in the house, I'd replay in my head conversations that we had shared. There were still a lot of questions I wanted answers to and I was sure I would get them in due course. I really hoped I would.

College was back and so were we. My assignment, for all my concern, wasn't so bad after all. I achieved a B, which for all my dithering around was a decent mark. I soon got into college routine. The guys continued their parenting role around me. I wondered when that would end or even if. How old would I have to be before their concern for my well-being would cease?

A couple of weeks passed and there was still no sign of Gabriel. When I had free time, especially at night, he was on my mind constantly. The visits I made to the diner had an ulterior motive. I was hoping he would be there, waiting to surprise me as he did before. I still hadn't mentioned him to Rob and Jamie yet. I think maybe I was thinking that there was going to be no need, especially when I hadn't seen Gabriel in such a long time. But secretly deep down I was really wishing there was; I missed him so much!

The weekend was fast approaching. Rob and Jamie had arranged to drive down to Newquay, a little town known for its great surfing waves, towards the bottom end of Cornwall. The boys were taking their girlfriends and that was their compromise for their involvement in the rave weekend planned. I was asked of course to go along; no, actually told, but I declined. It wasn't much fun being a gooseberry around them and I'm sure their girlfriends wouldn't appreciate me hanging around either. Not that they would say anything. But I don't think the boys thought that way. Does a man really know what a woman wants? Even Dad did his best to persuade me. I knew it bothered him to think I'd be stuck at home on my own. Anyway, little did they know, I had other plans. I was fed up feeling this way, waiting around. I was going to do something about this. As the saying goes, if the mountain won't come to Mohammed, then Helena would go see Gabriel!

I'd decided to go Saturday evening, not too late. I wasn't sure I would remember how to get there, especially if it was dark. However, I'd try and make it easier on myself by going as early as I could. Dad had made arrangements to go fishing down at Shaldon Bridge, a popular small place known for its angling. Eric had travelled up from Plymouth to spend the weekend there, so I knew he would be preoccupied and not wanting to know too much about what I was doing. Dad had offered me the car. He wouldn't be needing it; Shaldon was local. Little did he know that I was really grateful for the gesture. I hadn't thought about how I was going to get there.

Saturday had nearly come and gone. I'd done my shift at work and carried out my usual weekend routine, stripping beds, which produced a mound of washing. However, I loved Saturdays. Even though it was busy around the house, I really loved the smell and feel of freshly made beds. For some reason I always had my best sleep on a Saturday night!

As I climbed into the driver's seat of Dad's Audi I could feel tingling sensations around my shoulders and neck. I was feeling nervous again. All day I was questioning my reasons for doing this. Perhaps I was being foolish, maybe he didn't want to know; that's why he hadn't been around. These thoughts had been badgering me all day and they were in abundance now. I was a little surprised at myself really. This wasn't something I would normally do.

I wasn't a strong-minded person but I'd always been inquisitive about stuff, so I guess that's what got me to this point.

I took the drive steadily towards his house, for two reasons really: a) this was Dad's car and I didn't want to prang it or anything, and b) I really was only going on a vague memory of how to get to Gabriel's house. When you're a passenger, you don't seem to take things in, so I was putting snippets of things I'd remembered into place, which would hopefully guide me in the right direction. It wasn't long before I really felt I was on the right track. I knew I was close; the clearing ahead I remembered with great enthusiasm. The trees hung over each other forming an archway, and then at the top of the hill there was an opening and the trees disappeared.

The house stood in the clearing, surrounded by shrubbery. I imagined the surroundings looking fantastic in the height of summer when all the colours would be at their most magnificent. My stomach was bubbly at the thought of getting closer. I could feel the chilliness of the air all over my skin. And that final argument in my head, as I left the house. Am I doing the right thing?

Lights were on inside the house. Gabriel was home. My nerves now had really taken hold. My body felt frozen. I grabbed my jacket from the back seat as I made my way to the front door, still trying to reassure myself I was doing the right thing. That was strange. No signs of another car. I rang the bell as I strained to see through the glass in the front door for any signs of life. There was no answer. I rang the bell again, hoping to get some sort of a response. Why wasn't he answering? Had I done something wrong? I knocked on the door, as if this would make any difference. Maybe he was telling me something and I wasn't listening or didn't want to listen. I turned and made my way towards the car. I was disappointed, to say the least.

"Hello? Can I help you?" I heard a strong masculine voice from behind me. The voice did not sound familiar. I turned around.

"Yes, hi, I'm looking for Gabriel," I said as I walked towards the male figure that blocked the way to the inside of the house. My first observation of this man was that he was dressed very smartly, casual but matching. He wore no tie but a scarf kind of thing that he wore around his neck, like those guys wear when going hunting. It was the only similarity I could think of. I'd say from first glance he was probably in his fifties but I might have been wrong. I wasn't good with ages.

"Gabriel? Ah! Yes. He's not here."

"Will he be back soon?"

"I'm not sure when he'll be back."

"Right," I said, disappointed.

"You must be Helena. Is that right?"

"Yes, that's right." I looked in his direction, bemused.

"Gabriel has told me all about you," he said as I gave an embarrassed smile.

I wondered what he had told this person. "Sorry, but I don't know… You are?" I questioned.

"Yes, I'm sorry, how rude. My name is Sealtiel, Gabriel's father," he said as he offered me his hand.

"Oh, hi."

I smiled. My first impression was that Mr King wasn't exactly what I was expecting. Especially as Gabriel's portrayal of him was so distant. I pictured someone very different.

"Would you like to come in? You've come all this way. I could offer you a drink at least before you go?"

"Um, yes! That would be great, thanks."

I followed in behind him. I didn't want to be rude. I was again aware of the same impression as when I last stepped into this house with Gabriel. The light in the house seemed to follow you around. I forgot how cold it was in here as well, as I pulled my arms across my chest. I was glad I'd brought my coat.

Gabriel's father was very hospitable; charming in fact. I could see no resemblance to the character I had made up for myself after experiencing Gabriel's lack of interest in him. He seemed a perfect gentleman. We made polite general conversation but he managed to incorporate how I'd met Gabriel. I told him the basics, which seemed to interest him. My feelings were that he seemed like a really cool guy. Gabriel apparently was with his aunt as she had become ill suddenly. So he wasn't even around. That explained his lack of interest.

Mr King said he would pass on my regards and I said my farewell. I was convinced on having a second glance at the furniture on the way out that it was definitely antique.

"Thanks again, Mr King. See ya!" I called as I walked towards the car.

"You're very welcome, Helena. Please call again, anytime. I will let Gabriel know you called," I heard him say from behind me. I gave a wave of acknowledgement.

The light was fading now as I started my journey home, hoping I'd remember my way back. My thoughts turned back to my chance meeting with Gabriel's father. I had to admit he wasn't at all how I expected him to be. He seemed a real sweetie, not how I had imagined from Gabriel's description of him. I thought about the last time we had spoken and how Gabriel had explained his father's reluctance to spend time with him as a child. It painted a very cold picture of him so today had been a big surprise. However, Mr King wasn't the last thought in my head as I drove home, Gabriel was. I hadn't managed to admit it to myself before but I really missed him. His return could not come soon enough.

10

Reunited

Days passed very slowly, especially after my little encounter up at Gabriel's house. I hadn't heard a word from him. I thought his father would have told him I'd been there straight away, then he would contact me, but not a word. I felt sluggish, lacking in energy, uninterested in anything I was doing. It was almost as if the things I had done before counted for nothing, had no purpose. I managed to put on my happy face when the guys and Dad were around but my lack of joining in as I once did must have been noticeable. I thought that I would feel better rather than worse after the visit but here I was, not able to function properly. If only he would call. I couldn't understand it; surely his father had told him by now. I know his father had said he was looking after his aunt but surely he had a few minutes to catch up with me. So part of me wished I hadn't gone now.

It was surprising how quickly the last week had gone. Saturday was back again. Had it really been a week ago since I called up at the house? Hard to figure. I'd been asked to work a later shift today. Millie, one of the girls, asked if I would swap my shift. It wasn't a big deal anyway. It was not like I had anything else on.

It was a short shift anyhow. I decided to call into the diner on the way there, just in case the guys were about, but they weren't. It was actually quite dead in the cinema tonight. In fact I couldn't remember seeing that many people when I walked through town earlier.

"Hels, do ya wanna go early? It doesn't look like it's going to pick up tonight. You might as well go home. Me and Sam can hold the fort if there's a mass rush," Nick said.

There was no one that was in charge but he'd been here the longest, so I guess he was in the best place to make the decision. And he was right. It was dead in there tonight.

"Yeah, OK! You sure?"

"Hmm, let me think," he said, pulling his palms up and moving them around the room.

I really hated that, sarcasm, never knowing whether they were joking or not.

"OK, OK, only asking!" I said as I grabbed my stuff and left.

I'd brought the car. Dad was at home tonight. I walked across the beach front to where the car was parked. At certain times of the year, before the grockles arrive, you can park right up to the beach. I loved this time of year, when you could walk on the sands quite peacefully.

Not many locals ventured down here in the winter but then again I'm not sure they did in the summer either. That happens when you live near an attraction; you never use it. It's surprising how you take it for granted and yet thousands of people each year spend thousands visiting. Easter onwards in Teignmouth, much like any other seaside resort, was a very different place indeed. And in the winter, everything on the seafront would be battened down and seem like a ghost town. Great for the older generation but not so great for the rest of us.

However, a couple of years back, the locals were given a real treat. A globally successful band whose members had grown up here as boys decided to come home and do a gig. It was their way of saying thank you for the loyalty of their local fans but really the thanks was all ours. Standing here now on the promenade, I cast my thoughts back, remembering the wait in the queue that early morning to collect our tickets. People had started queuing the day before, sleeping overnight in their little makeshift tents. The excitement was overwhelming; the town and locals were buzzing, especially when the band decided to pay us a visit that morning. Local voices joined in as one with band members, some they had known since kids at school, to give a rendition of their best-known hits. The atmosphere was truly electrifying.

It was the biggest thing I could ever remember that had hit our little town. The buzz around the place that weekend was vibrant. People from all over the world came for the gig. The pubs were packed to capacity, recruiting friends, neighbours and any local who was willing to help out for the event, and they all did it with a smile on their face. The place was alive and the Den, a patch of grassed area near the seafront, was transformed for the whole weekend into a spectacular event. This was a gig not just for us, it was for our parents and yes, dare I say it, even our grandparents. And they even completed their part by queuing for hours on end, whilst their grandchildren worked, just so they too would get the chance to be a part of that special time. I think people just wanted to say, "Hi, thanks for coming back. We really appreciate the revenue you've brought to the town and, hey, we're now on the map!" We were now known in the States. Awesome! Even today, when I stand here looking out and remembering, I still smile. It was a gig to remember!

I let the car run idly, as the engine ticked over, waiting for the heater to stop blowing cold air through the grilles, until it was warm enough to clear the windscreen at least. The sea breeze was chilly tonight but the waters were calm. It was really peaceful sat here. I searched my bag on the passenger seat for my Nano. My music needed to be plugged in. It was a must. Dad's selection was, let's say, a little mature for my liking, even if it was a short drive. I stretched my right arm up to turn the interior light on, as I continued to rummage through my bag. Found it! I searched around the dashboard in the dimly lit space to connect my iPod.

Something caught my attention. I glanced up quickly. I was interrupted by white light all around me. I turned around to look in the back of the car. I wasn't sure why I did that. A single knock was heard and I turned around abruptly to see where it had come from.

Although I was inquisitive, my heart skipped a beat. A second knock sounded on the passenger window. I bent my head to see who was on the other side. I could see nothing. The light was too bright, blinding me. This was ridiculous. Who was it?

My brain was telling me, don't get out, but my curiosity got the better of me. I looked towards the passenger side as I peered over the top of the car from the driver side but there was nothing.

The light was so intense.

"Hello, Helena," a voice said from within the brightness. Fear gripped me as I heard it say my name. Although fearful for my safety at this point I also felt familiarity, like I somehow knew this!

"Who are you? I can't see you!"

And like a bulb the light had gone out, and just street lighting remained.

My eyesight was all over the place. Little white speckles were dancing around as I blinked several times to get my vision back to normal.

"Hello, Helena."

That voice again, so clear and so close. I felt a hand touch mine. My heart was pounding heavily, my breathing doing the same. I turned quickly, fear not needed. This touch I knew.

"Hi!" he said, as he grabbed for the other hand.

We just stood there for what seemed like an eternity but probably was only minutes. My rapid breathing remained as I stood in front of him. I couldn't speak. All those mixed emotions racing around me. Joy at him being here now, and anger a little at why, why had he not been in touch sooner? Had he not realised how much he meant to me?

"Gabriel!" My voice was timid and breathless.

He returned a smile. God! I'd missed that. There was a glow about him when he did that. I was surprised I hadn't noticed it before. It could almost be described as a halo etched around him. There was something else, though, that I felt from it. It almost spoke to me, although not one word was spoken between us. It was from within, communicating through our souls.

'Helena, I'm so sorry. I have no excuses."

My face dropped. It was as though all those feelings just made me remember how sad and lonely I had been all this time without him. I felt his hand touch my face, the warmth of his hands as they cradled my cold cheeks, my head willingly pushing towards his hand. I'd never felt these emotions before. I felt overwhelmed and out of control. I had a need to be closer to him but fear was gripping me too. My body was telling me, be open, let go, but my mind was saying, be careful, this may not be what you think it is. Don't make a fool of yourself. These feelings were so hard to control. I slowly looked up, my face still cradled there in his hand. His smile hadn't changed; it was still there. It was there to reassure me that he hadn't forgotten me and that he had returned, to me! His face drew in closer to mine, as he very gently placed a soft kiss on my cheek. My heart was pounding. My head was whizzing all over. My eyes stared desperately at him, longing for him to kiss me. Surely he knew how I felt. My whole being in this moment was out of control and the climax of the moment gripped me. My eyes were closed tight. I didn't want him to see how willingly I was his, unless he felt the same. His smell was so breathtaking, controlling but not in a bad way. Surely he felt this hunger that was there inside of me, desperately wanting to be released.

"Helena? I know. I feel it too."

He gently took my face in both his hands and looked deeply into my eyes.

"I've always felt it!" he whispered.

His touch was so soft but intense as his lips touched mine. I could taste the sweetness of his mouth and the tension in his arms as they wrapped around me. Breathe, breathe, my conscious mind was screaming at me. But my body felt limp, as if it was about to buckle from underneath me.

He had felt it! His body language proved that.

As he pulled away gently, my eyes opened to be greeted with such a radiant smile. Mine came automatically. I could still feel the explosive state between us, desperately wanting to be released as I sensed the frustration in him.

"Shall we go home?" he asked as he pointed to the open door of the car.

My smile could have easily matched his at that moment. I was beaming all over. He knew how I felt; this yearning for him was visible to both of us. This whole different life I had within me when he was around made me yearn for more. This affection I had for him was more than I'd ever known before. The power it had over me was intoxicating, driving me to demand more. This love, dare I say it, had an element of pain, which I was experiencing now as we resisted what our mind and bodies were telling us. Not that I had ever experienced it before but if it felt like this, then it must have been. And best of all, Gabriel felt this too. He always had.

11

Why

The journey home was swift, even though I tried my hardest to slow the journey. I wanted more time with him. No words were spoken. They weren't needed. The air in the car seemed to carry on where the moments we had before had stopped. The movement of his hand brushing across my hair and then down my cheek, as I tried to keep all these emotions intact at least to get us home safely without pranging the car, was enhancing the burning feeling within me. He seemed so different, having a certain intensity about him, as though the time he been away had made him realise there was something missing. I could feel the depth of his stare on me and a longing that wasn't there before. A track from my iPod started playing but I hadn't remembered that I'd actually connected it. I also tuned into something else that was strange. I watched the volume counter lower itself like magic on the dashboard. I don't think Gabriel noticed the difference in volume. He never mentioned it anyway. I just couldn't work out how it happened.

In no time the car was parked. Lights were still on in the house and I could visualise Dad sat in front of the TV, watching his saved programmes, peanut bags and beer cans all around him to keep him company.

But really my attention was fixed on the man sat here beside me, as the engine silenced.

"Helena?"

I turned towards him.

"Yes?"

"I was wondering, now that I'm back again, whether you'd like to spend the day together tomorrow?" he asked.

"Yeah, you bet. You don't think now you're back that I'm going to let you go?" I smiled. I was beaming inside and out.

"OK! Well, I don't know what you'd like to do. Have you got anything in mind?"

"Er, I'm not sure. Maybe some alone time would be nice? What do you think?" Once I had said it, I thought better of it. Maybe he didn't see us in that way.

I watched as he got out of the car and I followed suit. I realised that I hadn't seen his car around. I didn't see it down town and I never thought to ask before. But he assured me it was parked around the corner.

"I walked down, after I called at yours earlier. Your dad, Mike, told me you were at work. So I took a walk down."

"So, when did you get back then?" I asked.

"This morning."

"And your aunt. She's better now?"

He had a really puzzled expression on his face, as we both leant on the side of the car.

"Aunt! How did you know about that? It happened so suddenly, hence no time to explain. But how did you know?"

"You could have called me. I was going out of my mind, thinking all sorts."

"I know you're right, but I got caught up in the situation there and well, it happened so quickly, I didn't have time to think. My dad contacted me the night I dropped you off and told me about my aunt. Of course, when I saw her, I couldn't leave her alone, so I stayed. But I should have called. Sorry!"

"Yes, you should have." But I couldn't be angry with him.

"Anyway, how did you find out I was there?" he asked.

"Your father told me. I called in at the house, wondering why you hadn't been around. I thought I'd done something to upset you."

"Helena! That's just not possible," he said with a wry look on his face.

"Hey, don't start with all the compliments. You're in my bad books."

"OK, OK," he smirked.

"Considered told," he said, bantering with himself.

"Forgiven?" He shot me a pleading, smirky expression.

"Maybe. I'll think about it," I said, smiling.

"That's fair enough." He returned the smile.

I really had missed that! I thought about how comfortable he seemed to be with me now. Able to understand and join in the banter we were having. I felt by meeting again today that we had grown. It just felt natural, what we had.

"Anyhow, you said you saw my father? When was this?"

"Last Saturday evening." I filled him in on the whole story of my encounter with Mr King and my observations about him. He didn't comment on it further.

"You said he was at the house?"

"Yes. He looked like he was staying there. Why?"

"Oh, no, nothing. It's just that he never said he was coming, that's all."

Gabriel looked really puzzled. I sensed his concern at what I had said.

"Right. Well, he even gave me a grand tour of the house, again. Of course I didn't tell him you had already done that. He does seem like a really nice man."

"Hmm, well, it's strange, that's all. He never told me." It was clear he was not happy.

"So he never told you I had called then?"

"No!" It was an answer that he gave but it was clear he had something else on his mind. "Sorry, Hels! No, he didn't." He still had that faraway look on his face.

"Oh well! It doesn't matter now. So what about tomorrow then? Where shall we go?" I said, trying to change the subject and thinking maybe he'd snap out of it.

"How about a film and then perhaps something to eat afterwards? I haven't seen a film in ages. What do you say?" he asked.

"Yeah, why not."

"You sure? I know you work there and maybe you don't really want people you work with seeing us together."

"Why wouldn't I?" I was a little disappointed at his presumption of the way I thought about him. But come to think about it, he was right. Hadn't I behaved that way with Rob and Jamie? I hadn't even told them about Gabriel.

"OK. So I'll come by around three, OK?" he asked.

"Yeah, sure."

He turned towards me and once again cradled my face in his hands. As he stared into my eyes I felt overwhelmed by his protectiveness but also something else, something I hadn't felt before meeting him. I felt this strong emotional tenderness for a guy I really hardly knew.

And I was powerless to stop it.

"It's really great to be back. I missed you!" He smiled softly.

"Yeah, likewise."

My head was all over the place. It felt like a pressure cooker ready to explode. Hearing him say those words was the icing on the cake. It reassured me that I hadn't got it wrong, that the vibes between us were real.

"See ya!"

"Yeah, tomorrow, right?"

"Yeah."

As he bent to place a tender kiss on my cheek, I could feel his hot breath on my skin and the sweetness of his scent as he lingered there, his chin now resting on my neck. My head was buzzing, my senses out of control as I felt him so definitely there. I so badly wanted more, for him to let go of himself, to forget he was a good guy. But that wasn't going to happen; he was the good guy and that's why I fell for him in the first place.

And with that, the moment had passed and he was gone.

Dad was just where I'd said he'd be. Hogging the TV, flat out on the sofa, snacks and beers strewn around him.

"Hey, Dad, you OK?"

"Oh, hi, sweetheart," he said as he sat up in the couch. "I never heard you come in. Work OK?"

"Yeah, it's fine," I said as I plonked myself in the chair opposite.

"I didn't realise it was that late."

"It's not, Dad. I left early. It was dead tonight, so they let me go early."

"Oh, right." He was still preoccupied with the TV.

"I'm going up. Do you want anything before I go?" I grabbed my stuff.

"No, you're all right. I'm fine."

"Hey! I forgot. That chap, Gabriel, is it? Well, he called, er, maybe around teatime for you. I told him you were working."

I turned around and retreated back to where he was sat.

"Yeah, I know. We met down town."

"Oh, OK. I wasn't sure what was happening. I haven't seen you around with him much lately," he said questioningly.

"Yeah, he's been away."

"You know, I'm sure I've seen him before. He looks so familiar."

"Nah! Don't think so, Dad. He hasn't lived around here since he was a boy."

"Hmm! Oh well, I could have sworn."

"Dad, I'm going now."

I started for the stairs again.

"OK," he said as he returned to his previous position in front of the TV.

That's twice now he's mentioned it, I thought as I lay in the bath. My head was buzzing, filled with memories of the last hour. Gabriel had been so different, more open. And I wasn't expecting that. But I liked it all the same.

There was an excitement in me that I hadn't felt in a long while but even then, it was never like this. This I hadn't ever felt. It was intensifying and I was having difficulty controlling what was inside. These emotions were so powerful and in a strange way, frightening. If I felt this much emotion when all was going well then what would it be like if it wasn't? I shook my head. Not a thought I cared to dwell on. A shiver escaped down my neck. I shifted my weight down into the bath as the warmth completely diminished any thoughts I had.

Book Two

Gabriel

12

Bonding

The moon was bright tonight. I couldn't help but look up; it was almost full. The walk to the car was brief. Stuff was on my mind. Things Helena had said earlier. How long had he been there? Why hadn't he said anything? He knew I was going down to Cornwall. So why didn't he hang around until I got back? He knew it would wind me up.

That was typical of him. He had a habit of doing that. Trying to push his way into my life when things were going well. It was as if he hated me being happy at anything. Thinking back, that was probably most of the time. I'd always been aware my Aunt Ezra had had no time for my father. She made it perfectly clear, especially when he would make the odd visit to see me. She'd make her exit. I thought at first she was just doing it to give us some space but as I got older I could read between the lines and that certainly wasn't the case. It was strange; it was almost like she had real hatred towards him. But she would never say anything about him in front of me. And as it was as I got older, his visits became fewer. I can't say I was that bothered anyway. He wasn't exactly a hands-on father. He never gave me the sit-down talks that most parents would do with their kids, and the father-and-son quality time that I watched other parents give their children was definitely out. There was none of that from him. Hence the lack of a bond between us now. However, the reason for my returning here was mainly down to his influence. He had a way of making me feel like a total loser when I came up against him, inadequate. I loved the life I had with my aunt. It was uncomplicated. She had always lived a single life, so when I came along she was so appreciative. To her I was a big part of her life, and to me I guess I was her son. She was a simple woman, a warm and gentle person, all the things a young boy would need without his real mother around. It was just a happy time. However, when he turned up somehow he managed to spoil it by saying something that would make me feel like crap and then I would watch an expression of sheer hate creep over my aunt's face. But she never said a word, not one. She was my mother's sister, her only sister, so I believe. My aunt would tell me endless stories of her and my mother and how close they were as kids, even right up to the time of my mother's death. As I got older I could recognise the sadness that probably had always been there in my aunt's eyes, as she talked about her. Before too long, the time came for me to think about moving on. The decision was partly down to wanting to spite him. Although I'm not sure he really cared enough anyway for it to make the slightest bit of difference to him.

But I wanted to make a stand, telling him, look I can do this without you, I can live on my own and, yes, I can cut the apron strings that you so often remind me of.

I really hadn't thought it through. Moving back into the house was going to be a physical challenge. It had been empty for quite some time, so it was in desperate need of some life to give it character. My father moved out many years ago, just upped and left, leaving everything as it was. Separating from my aunt felt a lot worse for her I think. For me it was an adventure; that's how I saw it. For her it must have been a lot worse, although she never said. But then she wouldn't have done; it just wasn't her way. I invited her to come and stay but she always refused. Too many memories, I guess.

The drive home was swift. Thoughts of him were still irritating me when I pulled up, niggling away at me. I think knowing that I couldn't have a go at him about it was irritating me all the more. Contact was always on his terms. I would just have to wait it out. It was good to be back here but I had to confess, meeting up with Helena today was a bit nervy. I just wasn't too sure how it was going to play out. I was expecting it to be a lot worse and to be honest, if the boot was on the other foot, so to speak, I think I would have got really pissed about it. I knew I got away with it very lightly. In fact, she was really understanding about it, actually. It showed what great character she had. I liked that about her. But I was also aware that Helena had a vulnerable side to her. The night in the station was a good example of that. I was able to sense that fear running through her that night and yet I didn't even know her. How was that possible? These questions I couldn't answer but I knew she wanted answers. I didn't know why I needed to be there that day at the station but it almost felt as though I was being guided there. I had no recollection of how I came to be there, as I didn't the next couple of times we met. It was as though those memories were erased and I wasn't able to piece things together.

I just didn't have any answers.

I needed to do a few things today before meeting up with Helena later. I didn't work; never had to. I was told from a very young age that it wasn't fitting for me to do manual labour, that no member of the family had ever worked for money. The upkeep of the house would be sorted by my father. It wasn't my concern. I was given an allowance each month from my father and my mother had the foresight to look after my future. I'd come to accept this kind of life now but growing up, especially around my teenage years, I found it really difficult to accept. People of my age were either working or in university. But it wasn't just about the money. It was more than that;

I missed growing up with people. Now at the age of twenty-five I'd got used to this way of life without any more questions. When I thought about it, my life from as far back as I could remember was always sheltered. I couldn't remember having gone to school and yet I was educated, had not had to go to work, but had money.

At times, these things puzzled me. My aunt would tell me it was because I was special. But then she would say that, wouldn't she? But it never really answered my questions. I glanced at my watch as I sat there writing a letter to my aunt. I needed to hurry. There wasn't one clock in this house that worked. My father told me they were ancient, that they were meant to be that way. Who was I to argue?

As I pulled up outside Helena's house, I quickly checked myself. I had decided to wear something more casual, although I don't remember even changing, which was odd. I shook my head at the thought. Anyway, hopefully she'd think I looked OK. Clothes had always been a formal thing, right from being a small boy. I had never had mates to get ideas from so I knew no different. I always thought that was a little weird. So in a sense, this whole socialising thing was like being reborn.

"Hey!" she said, as she jumped into the car.

"Hi," I replied, trying to sound a little more hip. I was conscious that sometimes my way of saying things didn't always seem to fit. I guessed the socialising thing would help with that in time.

"You OK?" she asked, whilst giving me the once-over. "Wow, you look great," she said as she stared.

I was actually feeling a little weird, maybe a little self-conscious. I had the urge to look away with embarrassment, maybe because I liked what she had said but didn't know how to reply.

I hadn't felt like this before, but then again nobody ever noticed me like that before. But maybe this was normal for a guy to feel this way?

"You look nice too," I said, paying back the compliment. I was not sure whether this was how it was done but Helena seemed to take it in a good way.

"Shall we go, then?" she replied.

"Yeah."

We made for the town.

I didn't attempt to grab her hand as we climbed out of the car. I didn't want her to feel awkward in front of her workmates. I thought I really wanted to. The entrance, as we walked into the cinema, was fairly empty. Which was kind of good, being this was my first time ever.

I had told her I hadn't been for a while because I didn't want her questioning it. After all it was kind of weird. Most people have been to the cinema in their life. I watched as a girl made her way towards us and Hels walked slightly ahead to greet her. I watched them as I wondered whether all people greet each other in this way. This hugging of each other seemed a really nice way to say hello. Do men do this too? A question to ask Hels later. I couldn't really hear a lot of what was said. I stayed back, not wanting to cramp her style. They both looked in my direction and then returned to their conversation. The billboards were fascinating, full of life, energy and colour. I was truly amazed by them as I walked around the entrance area, absorbing all the information. It wasn't long before Helena had returned and we were heading down through this long corridor with more colourful faces on the walls.

Helena took the lead through the double doors, pulling me through behind her. I was surprised how dark it was in here, my eyes automatically drawn to the massive bright object that now stood in front of me, as Helena guided me into a seat. This was magnificent! I was overwhelmed by its size and how it drew you in, as if you were a part of it somehow. I'd never seen anything like it before.

81

"You OK?" Helena whispered to me.

"Yes, it's fabulous."

"Sshh, not so loud."

I glanced away from the huge screen to look at her.

"What?"

Helena gave me a quizzical look.

"You have to whisper. Others behind us can't hear."

She pointed behind us. I got it straight away.

"Right sorry," I said as I returned my attention to the screen. The noise was spellbinding.

"If I didn't know better, I'd think this was the first time you'd been to the pictures," I heard her say.

"Hmm." I said nothing more as I glanced back in her direction before returning my attention to the cinema screen. If only she knew!

13

Reason

All the way out, I never stopped talking. Not about the film but about the make-up of it. It was amazing!

"Gabriel! I was only joking," Helena said as we jumped into the car.

I wasn't sure what she was saying.

"What were you only joking about?" I asked as I turned the key in the ignition.

"You know, the first time thing," she said.

I was totally confused.

"The cinema, the first time you had been, I mean," she explained.

"Oh, I see. Well, actually it was!"

"What! You're joking, right? But you said…" She stopped, as though she realised it just didn't matter any more. She just threw me a quizzical look instead, not sure whether or not I meant it.

As I released the handbrake, I threw her a smile in return. Life couldn't be much better than it was right now!

Hels picked a place to eat. She said it was quiet, somewhere we could talk. She took us to a little place some ways off from Teignmouth itself, a place called Bishopsteignton. A small pub sat in the middle of the village. It was the only one here; it had the same amenities as any other pub but it had a really quaint feel to it. It reminded me of some of the places I'd seen driving around Cornwall; very pretty. We found a place to sit over in the corner of the room, tucked away in the back. It was dark in there. The ceiling had low level beams everywhere, giving it a historic feel.

"Well, now that you've got me here, what do you plan to do with me?" It was a quote I'd memorised from the film we'd just seen.

Helena shot me a look. "Hmm, let me see," she said as she rubbed her hands together over the table. The look she threw me told me she'd remembered too.

We both burst out laughing as we realised. Helena ordered our meals and drinks from the bar as I handed her the cash. At one point I wasn't sure whether or not I should have ordered myself; she seemed to be giving me this strange look as I handed her the money.

But I'm sure she would have told me if that was the case. I watched her as she returned with the drinks and what Helena called a receipt, as she placed it in my hand. A square piece of paper with printed black ink written all over it. This was new to me. I hadn't seen anything like this before. I very rarely bought anything for myself, and when I did I never hung around for a receipt. I didn't realise I had to. What was I supposed to do with it? I offered her back the piece of paper.

"You need to keep that. Payment for the things I just ordered," she explained, really looking questioningly at me now.

"Oh, right, yes, of course," I said as I made out I knew but just had memory loss.

"So, Gabriel? Are you going to tell me what your father said? Why he was here?"

"There's nothing to tell. I haven't spoken to him yet."

"Really. I thought after our conversation last night, it would be the first thing you would have done."

"He's not the easiest of people to get hold of. In fact I will have to wait until he contacts me."

"That's strange though, don't you think?"

"What's strange?" I asked.

"The fact he hasn't tried to get in touch or leave a note or anything. You'd think he would have at least done that," she said.

"Helena, my father's not exactly my closest of companions," I explained.

"Nevertheless, close or not he was in your house whilst you were away. At least he could have asked."

"Technically, that house is his. And I'm the last person he would ask permission to do anything."

"I'm really surprised. He seemed such a nice guy when I met him up at the house."

"Hmm, well, you don't know him."

At that moment a woman in black clothing with a white apron draped around her waist appeared with two plates in her hands. She addressed Helena with a question about where to place these items. Hels pointed to the empty place mat in front of me.

"Enjoy your meals," she said as she placed the plate down in front of me. She never addressed me at all. She looked at Helena for acknowledgement before taking her leave. That was weird! I felt as if I was looking from the outside in, like I was inside a bubble and it was going on around me. Strange!

"Is your meal OK?" Helena asked.

I was still thinking about the previous situation.

"Yeah, fine!" Although I said so, I wasn't too sure what just went on there.

The afternoon whizzed by. The conversation was good between us, although I think Helena contributed to it more than me. I still had the previous situation in my mind, which I guess caused some distraction. Hels had a notable query – why I hadn't touched my food and drink. I just wasn't hungry; that was all. Sometimes when we talked, I would get so engrossed in all her storytelling that I'd lose track of time. She made it sound so exciting.

It wasn't late when we decided to go home but Helena pointed out that she was in college early the next day. I wondered about that. What it was like to study and be with other people. One day I would ask her.

The moments in the car were the most intoxicating, being around her. The small confined space urging me to get closer. I wasn't always sure what she was thinking, leaving me feeling emotionally vulnerable. Sometimes she would throw me this look that I just couldn't understand, and other times I was able to see right through her, hear all of her thoughts, even the ones she didn't want me to know. I stopped the car outside her house. A part of me was a little disappointed to get here already.

"I had a really great time today," I said, smiling.

"Yeah, me too. It was fab!" She returned my smile.

I couldn't help but stare at her. She was so beautiful. Her deep blue eyes and raven black hair enhanced the features in her face. My body wanted to grab her up and kiss her fully on the lips, take ownership of her. But something in my mind said wait, maybe this is not what you think this is. Don't push too fast, not now that you have found it.

I placed one hand on her cheek. My fingers were so eager to touch her as her warmth raged through my body, and I moved forward to place my face against hers and kissed her cheek. I lingered there for a few seconds, her smell embracing me. I felt a hand cover mine on her cheek, as a sense of more heat surrounded my body. I really wanted her! Hunger within me was raging but I knew I needed to tame this passion right now. I pulled away gently to look into her eyes. I wanted to see what she was feeling right at that moment. Were we the same, her and me? Did we feel the same things? And right now, was I reading the right signs? Her eyes said yes!

And as quick as it came, I had to let the moment go. Let her leave this car even though this was the last thing in my mind, but it was necessary right now. She grabbed her stuff and was soon on the outside of the car, peering in through the passenger window.

"See ya!" she whispered, as she looked into my eyes, as though she was trying to rekindle the moment.

"Yeah, see ya," I replied, and watched her disappear into the house.

Thoughts of the day played over and over in my mind as I drove home. All these feelings, emotions, trapped in this body, desperately trying to escape and fulfil their true potential. Questions, so many of them, unanswered. New in my experience, today and the other days since meeting her. And old ones, ones I'd asked myself before but got no real answers. Questions that had been locked away for many years but had come back. Back for answers. And now my experiences could reveal those answers.

A couple of days went by. Helena was presumably at college and I was here at home alone. Never before had I questioned what I done with my days in this house. It's funny, until all of this, before Hels, what did I do with my time? Time hadn't been a problem before but now it seemed to be either moving too slowly or too fast.

I was conscious I was constantly trying to fill the void of time now. And yet before it never even entered my head. I couldn't remember what I used to do with my days, or evenings come to that. It was as though all the recent changes had awakened something in me. There was never the need before. I was content with just being. But things had changed. She had done that.

I wanted to see her. No, I needed to see her. I would call her tonight. I knew she had planned to meet up with her two friends this evening, but I would wait for her and see her later. I didn't know how I knew about her plans, but I did. And thinking that now seemed strange to me. It was so hard to understand, as I searched within myself for answers, but there were none. I thought to call her or text her but then thought better of it. A surprise was always better.

I watched as Helena walked towards her house. I knew she was coming. I could feel her presence. There was surprise on her face as she glanced up from the ground, idly walking up the hill, and the stretched smile that was etched on her face just showed me what I already knew – she was happy to see me. My body was flowing with strong emotional wanting again and so difficult to control in front of her. Her pace quickened and my first instinct was to throw out my arms and wrap them around her, like she had done with her friend at the picture house, but my caution stopped me. I couldn't be sure how it would be received. Sometimes I questioned my reasoning for the decisions I made about her. I could feel her emotions. I'd always been able to do that, right from the moment I saw her. So why was I questioning what I already knew, or was it me that I was reasoning with? I knew there had been a difference in me. I sensed that from the moment I came back. But there were things I didn't understand about myself, that I needed to feel sure about first before I made the commitment.

"Hey you!" I heard her say as she continued to climb the steady slope, her smile still beaming. "You OK?" she continued as she stretched out her arms and threw them around my neck.

It was my turn to be surprised. I didn't know what my approach should be. My body wanted to react but my reasoning was doing its thing, my arms still stuck to my sides. I wanted to match her embrace so badly, my fingers itching to fold around her body. Would that be so wrong?

"It's so great to see you, Gabriel," she whispered in my ear.

Her hot breath on my neck seemed to linger there forever. The smell of her perfume felt intoxicating to my very being.

"Are you alright?" She was still whispering. She hadn't let go yet.

My arms still hung at my sides, wrestling with my reasoning.

She relaxed her grip. I looked deep into her eyes. I sensed a strangeness in them. I couldn't quite work it out. It was like she was questioning something that she didn't understand.

"Yeah, I am now!"

Her smile was so gentle as I followed her into the house.

14

The Meeting

I stretched out my arms over the top of the steering wheel. Today was a good day! In fact, every day now was a good day. Although I never actually said anything to Helena about my emptiness at home, now somehow she knew. And so she came up with the idea that I could pick her up from college and I would listen to her tell me all about her day.

We saw each other as often as we could; after work, after college, at the weekend, any spare time that was possible. And I now had my purpose! Hels would constantly go on about the weather and how warm it was. For some reason she seemed to thrive on the thought of it. I asked her once why it was such a big deal. After all weather was weather, no big thing surely. She just said, "Gabriel, you serious? Look at it all. It makes you feel great. The sun when it shines on your skin makes you feel good and the heat just warms right through you, like a cosy blanket. Surely you feel that? You must do!"

I remembered thinking about that, at what she had said, how she described it. And honestly, hand on heart, no, I didn't. I mean, I could see the physical change in the weather, going through the seasons, but I honestly couldn't feel the difference. The whole thing was strange to me, I just didn't get it. It was clear from taking note that the changes in the seasons required changes with what people wore or didn't wear. And I would need to adapt to this.

Helena wanted us to go to the diner tonight. She didn't say why but it was clear something was on her mind. If anything she had been a little quiet, distant even. Not her usual bubbly self. When I asked, she just said she was fine but I got the feeling that wasn't the case. I hadn't seen her all day. She'd arranged to bring herself back from college, saying she was using her dad's car, as he was away for a few days. Some conference or something. She would collect me later. I was conscious she hadn't been here for a long while, not since she met with my father. Thinking about it again still made me mad. My father did eventually contact me weeks after I returned from my aunt's and he was his usual self, making snide comments about my stay with her.

I really hated that! He was also very flippant about his stay at the house whilst I was away, as if it was no concern of mine what he did or didn't do, and where for that matter. He made it abundantly clear that it was his house and I was just passing through. Just another passing comment from him to leave me feeling no affection for the man. I asked him about Helena and why he hadn't contacted me when she visited. He just said, "Hmm, well…" and that was it, as if he stopped in mid-thought, saying no more on the subject. Of course I lost patience with him and abruptly cut the conversation short in my annoyance. I briefly mentioned it in conversation to Helena but she didn't really make any comment on it. I guess she just read my expression and that gave her enough understanding of the situation. There was no reason to say any more.

I was ready and waiting for her. In fact, I'd been waiting all day. I had done my best in adopting the casual look again with my clothes. I hoped Helena would appreciate it. It was something she never commented on, what I wore, so I guess she was fine with the choices I made. My emotions were running high again, waiting here for her. Excitement sure, but there was something else; nervousness maybe.

And perhaps this was from waiting around. It obviously didn't suit me. Normally I'd insist on being the one to collect; waiting around was definitely a nervy process. I wondered whether or not Helena felt this way. I paced the room, which seemed like only minutes but probably was in actual fact most of the evening. And then I caught the back end of her car through the window. She was here at last! I crossed the room to greet her at the door.

She looked great! I took on board what Helena had said about the changes in the weather, by wearing something less formal, and she also demonstrated the changes herself. She looked really good.

"So, where we going?"

"The diner. I thought it was time you met up with my friends and them you," she explained, as the engine of the car turned over.

"But I've already done that," I reminded her.

"Not officially with me."

"Oh! Right," I said with a smile as she drove off.

She wanted to introduce me to her friends. This would be interesting. In fact, probably embarrassing. She'd obviously planned this, so I wondered in what context she'd described me to them. The diner was packed tonight but we managed to find a place to sit in view of the entrance. The guys hadn't got here yet. If I was being honest, I was beginning to feel a little nervous about the whole meeting thing. What if I did something wrong, said the wrong thing? What if they didn't like me? Maybe that would affect how she saw me and our friendship? I guess I'd soon find out.

"It's a little busier than the last time we were here," I pointed out.

She looked around as she got comfy, taking a sip of her drink.

"Yeah, you're right. It is really busy in here tonight."

"In fact it's been a while since I was last in here."

She turned in my direction.

"I wonder why?" she said with a smile.

I returned the gesture.

Conversation between the two of us was a little distracted. Helena took note of her watch every few minutes. Although she tried to look interested in the topics we discussed, she was clearly somewhere else. She was fidgety, checking the entrance every time the door opened. I could sense she was anxious. I knew she wanted this meeting but she seemed worried all the same. She never spoke about her friends much but I knew they were a big part of her life, important to her, so I needed to care about what she thought about this situation. I needed to show my support. I cupped my hands over hers, as they jumped up and down in the middle of the table, as if she had a nervous twitch. She seemed wound up, like a coiled spring. I'm sure that if the guys walked in at just that moment and my hands let go, her body would have bolted up in a coiled reaction. She was wound so tight! I thought better of bringing attention to this. I just kept our conversation going, hoping to gain some of her attention again. We'd waited long enough to have two hot drinks and then some. In fact Helena had drunk both the drinks herself. I wasn't particularly thirsty. I glanced at my watch for recollection of the time. We'd been here almost an hour already. I had no idea what time they'd planned to meet. She had not mentioned it.

"I know. They're really late!" she stated.

"So what time did you say to be here?" I asked.

"About six."

I remembered the time on my watch. Only twenty minutes late by my reckoning. That didn't seem too bad; well, not to be in the state she was in at any rate.

"I'm sure there's a really good reason anyway," I said with a reassuring smile, trying to grab her attention.

"Yeah," she said, but her attention was still on the entrance door.

Over the din of the other people in the room, I caught the faint tone of some kind of music. It was coming from Helena but she was still transfixed by the door.

"Helena. Helena." I tried to get her attention over the clanking of cutlery and other noise around us.

"Uh?" She turned swiftly to face me.

My hand pointed to her jacket pocket. "Your phone."

"My cell. Oh!" she exclaimed as she sprang into life and grappled with her pocket in time to answer her phone.

"Hi, where are you?" she answered anxiously.

She snapped the phone shut seconds later, as she studied the details on the screen. The conversation seemed one-sided.

"Who was that?" I asked.

She was still studying the screen.

"Rob I think but…"

She had been cut off. The phone rang again, and Helena flipped up the front of the screen.

"It's a message. He's going to be late; another twenty minutes," she said, closing down the shutter on her phone.

"Anything wrong?" I asked.

"I don't know; he didn't say." Helena's body tension changed from rigid to more relaxed, but her face still had a slightly worried look on it.

"I'm sure they're alright, Hels," I said, trying to reassure her.

She smiled to note my comment.

We made small talk but it was clear her mind was elsewhere. Twenty minutes came and went and she was getting fidgety again, grabbing her phone from the table.

"I think I'll phone. I can't understand what's keeping them. It's been ages! Something must be wrong."

I said nothing but nodded in agreement.

She searched her phone list and made the connection.

"Nothing. Just his answer machine," she said, and left her message. "Maybe he's got no signal. I'll leave a text." She started to thumb the keypad. With a sudden start, she jumped up from her seat, phone in hand and made for the entrance, and I could only watch as her tension turned to sheer joy at the sight of her friend walking through the doorway. I stayed where I was, watching from afar, as Helena greeted one of her friends. They were both clearly pleased to see each other, doing that hugging thing as she had done with her work colleague at the cinema that time. I watched as Helena's expression turned from happy to sad all in a short space of time. I could instantly feel the pain she now felt and the concern that was building within her. The conversation between them seemed to be really fraught and anxious. There was clearly something not quite right. I sensed her tension release a little, as she pointed in my direction and her friend followed her gaze, only for them to return to their conversation as before the next moment. They stayed a short while at the entrance and then he was gone and Helena made her way back towards me. The tension I felt from her had a strange edge to it. Yes, there were strong feelings of concern, worry and so on, but there was something else. I couldn't explain it, maybe because I didn't understand it, but there was definitely something upsetting her. She reached the table and took her seat.

"You OK? Everything OK?" I asked, noting the concern written on her face.

There was silence for a moment.

"Helena?"

I placed a hand on hers, as they lay cupped on the table. She seemed preoccupied somewhere else.

"Helena?"

She suddenly broke from her trance.

"Yeah?" she said as she stared at me. I sensed a strange feeling from her, as though there was some meaning behind it. I was confused.

"Is everything alright?" I think her behaviour was rubbing off on me. Even I was beginning to feel concerned. However, I didn't know who for. She eventually snapped out of her dream state but she still didn't seem to be herself.

"It's Jamie." She gently pulled her hand away from mine.

"What's Jamie? What's wrong?"

Her body tension softened slightly.

"He's in hospital. Involved in some kind of car accident," she said, still looking a little preoccupied.

"But what about Rob? He looked…"

She cut me off. "He's fine; a few cuts and bruises but he'll be OK. I need to go see him," she informed me.

"Of course. Would you like me to come with you? I can drive you," I offered as she started to leave.

"No! It's fine. Rob is picking me up in an hour."

Her answers were rather abrupt, or so I thought, and a little confusing. Something wasn't right but I just couldn't fathom it out. The conversation between us on the way back to my place was noticeably strained and really restricted to yes and no answers. Watching her as she drove I could feel how focused she was. My senses were doing overtime. Pain and anguish but also annoyance, confusion and scepticism were all in there, grinding away at her. Within minutes we were stationed outside my house.

"Helena, are you OK? Have I done something wrong to upset you?"

She turned to look at me. I noted a strangeness in her eyes, mellow but questioning. There was definitely something not right here.

"Yes, I'm fine. It's just that…"

I cut her off. "I know. I'm sorry for your pain but I'm sure he'll be alright," I said as I tried to reassure her.

She looked as if she was daydreaming.

"Helena?"

She snapped back again.

"Yes. I'm sure you're right."

"Will I see you later?" I asked as I climbed out of the car.

"Yes, later."

She selected the right gear and then she was gone.

I stood in the porch as I watched her disappear from view. This strangeness I felt had a tinge of concern to it, but I realised it wasn't concern for her friend or herself but rather for me. Something had changed her and it had been since she had spoken to Rob.

But what could they have possibly spoken about that had changed things so much? In that moment, what had gone wrong?

15

Confusion

"Hello, Gabriel."

The figure of a woman loomed over me as I lay still in my bed. I didn't move at all but I wasn't frightened. I just stayed there, looking up at her. My eyes were still full of sleepiness as I rubbed them to get a clearer look. A yawn escaped from my mouth as my face was still nuzzling the pillow.

"Auntie?"

The woman bent closer to me. She didn't smell like Auntie. I would have known her smell anywhere. It was all warm and cuddly. No, this was more scented; adventurous, but private. I watched as her long black hair tumbled around her shoulders and surrounded her face. I couldn't see her face properly. It was so dark that the shadow from her hair blocked it out. It was as though she had read my thoughts, for she extended her hand to pull her hair from one side of her face.

"No, I'm not Auntie," she said to me with a smile. She was pretty.

"Who are you then?" I asked as I pulled myself up to rest my head on the headboard.

She touched my hand. Her skin was soft, not like Auntie soft, all wrinkly and hanging, but smooth-soft, and it didn't move when you touched it.

"I'm your mother, Gabriel," she announced softly.

"My mother? But you can't be; you don't smell like her," I said, still sleepy.

"You are right, Gabriel. Auntie loves you so much but I am your real mother," she said with a smile.

"You are? But how? I thought you died?" I was not frightened of her. In fact she was really nice and I really liked how she smelled; not as good as Auntie but I liked it.

"I have come here now because you need me, and when you need me again, I will be here for you. I wanted you to know this," she explained.

"Will you be here in the morning when I wake up?" I was starting to feel my eyes getting heavy again.

"No, Gabriel. Only when you need me. Your aunt loves you and she will take care of you until that time," I heard her say, as my eyelids closed over. "Gabriel, I love you more than you will ever come to know. You are a most special boy and one day you will come to know that." Her voice was distant.

"Mummy, do you love me?"

"Gabriel, I will always love you. You are my beautiful boy. Always remember this."

"OK, Mummy, love you," I said as my body slipped down and I drifted back to sleep.

I felt the jerk of my body as I came to realise where I was. I must have fallen asleep on the bed. I tried to collect my thoughts, as I felt a little all over the place. Helena had dropped me off before going to the hospital. I remembered that but after that I was a bit confused. How long had I been home?

The light through the window indicated that it was still daylight. I glanced at my watch. It was nine thirty in the morning. I'd slept right through. I grabbed my phone from the bedside cabinet. She must have called and I'd slept through it, I thought. On checking the calls, I found nothing to indicate that I'd missed any. She hadn't called. I walked towards the front door, thinking maybe she'd put a note through the letterbox. But again there was nothing. Strange! Maybe she thought it was too late to get in contact by the time she'd finished. I glanced at my watch again. It was too late to ring her. She'd be at college now. I'll make a visit to hers tonight when she gets home, I thought. I tried to call her, when I knew her classes were due to finish, just to let her know I would be calling over. I thought I could give her some support that night if she was planning on visiting. But her phone seemed to be switched off. She must have forgotten to switch it back on again when leaving college. I tried to think positively, but just like the day before something was nagging at me as if I was missing something.

I tried not to think too much about it as I jumped into the driver's seat of the car. I was sure all this strangeness had an explanation. I took a long interesting look at the sky through the windscreen as I drove, like I'd never done before. I thought of the times Helena had mentioned how the changes in the weather made you feel differently. The sky almost seemed like a picture unfolding. The fluffiness of the clouds, and the gaps where a brighter colour desperately tried to shine through and the edging of the fluffiness was much brighter, was almost hurtful to the eyes as I stared, mesmerised by its magnificence. Rays of bright light seeped through the gaps, forming a fan-like effect. She was right. The weather did hold some fascination.

I reached Helena's house in a very short time. Her father's car sat in the driveway. I looked for signs of life through the Sachs curtains drawn at the windows as I rang the doorbell. It rang several times with no acknowledgement. Strange. Maybe they'd gone out and left the car behind. As I made my way back to the car, I spied movement from the side of the house and Helena's father appeared from behind the gate.

"Hey! Can I help you?" he said.

"Hello. Yes, I'm looking for Helena."

He made his way towards me.

"Yes, you're Gabriel, aren't you?"

"Yes, that's right. I just wondered if Helena was in."

"No. She's with her friend. Rob, you know?"

"Yeah. So have I just missed her then?"

"No, no. She stayed over his house last night."

I was a little bit taken aback by his last comment. I certainly wasn't expecting it and I didn't know why but I felt an instant tightness in my chest. My body was tingling with uneasiness. It definitely wasn't a good feeling.

"Right." I was confused. Why didn't she tell me?

"I think they're going to see Jamie in hospital tonight. Perhaps you can meet up with them there."

"Maybe! Might you know the visiting times?" I asked.

"Of course. Hang on a minute; I'll get them."

As I sat in my car contemplating my actions, uneasiness and confusion really played their part with me. Why hadn't she said anything last night about staying over? In fact, why hadn't she phoned me today? She must have realised I would be worried.

I was distracted by a knock on the driver's window. Mike had returned.

"Are you alright, son? Here you go. All the details are here," he said as he handed me a piece of paper, sensing, I guess, that I was a little distracted.

"Yes, of course, Mr Garrett. I'm fine."

I smiled, hoping it would ease his concern.

"You know, I could have sworn I'd seen you some place before," he said, as I sensed he was investigating me.

"As I said before, Mr Garrett, I haven't lived around here for such a long time."

"Your family, are they locals?"

"Yes, they've lived here for many years. I say lived, but I mean that now in the past tense. My father moved away some time ago."

"And what about your mother?" he asked, looking rather intrigued.

"Well, my…"

I was cut off abruptly. His hands gestured that he had heard something.

"Sorry, son. I need to get that," he said as he dashed towards the shrilling tone of the phone that was now ringing in the house. "I'll tell her you called," he shouted back at me, and then he was gone.

I managed to find my way to the hospital ward. It was surprisingly easy, considering I'd asked no one for directions.

Everywhere seemed busy. Professionals in their starched uniforms, holding large clipboards, discussing patients' symptoms with others whilst they huddled around their stations. Visitors making idle chit-chat, trying to keep their loved ones' spirits high whilst they lay in hope that they could go with them when they left, feeling trapped by their illnesses.

As I entered the ward, I was surprised at how quiet it was; peaceful even. This was the first time I could remember being in a place like this. And it was strange but somehow soothing. I watched as patients' faces changed to sheer joy when their visitors arrived at their bedsides and felt a great surge of wellness, as if to prove they were ready to go home. I continued to watch several scenes like these as I passed through the different departments in the ward, and I still hadn't found Helena in any of them. I could see I was nearing the end and I noted my chest was starting to feel heavy.

As I turned a corner, I caught sight of Helena's friend Jamie as he lay restfully in a bed. He was asleep. And he had no visitors yet. His leg was pulled up in some kind of contraption and the opposite arm, which lay on top of his chest, was covered in thick casting. His face had colour shadings of blacks, browns and yellows. Not knowing the details of his accident, I thought he looked like he'd been lucky to come out of it alive. I stood for a moment, admiring him for how peaceful he seemed lying there. The tightness in my chest had noticeably worsened and my stomach felt like something was moving around in there. Not heavy, but light and fluffy.

I glanced around the room at the other three beds. Two were occupied with sleeping patients, and the other was empty. I was fascinated by the uniformity of design; how the beds sat in the position of what looked like the same distance apart from each other, and how the empty one had been made up for the next victim, all neat and packaged with its very tidy folded corners. I heard the clatter of what was presumably a tea trolley as it made its rounds through the ward, and the soft chatter of people in conversation as they got closer. Then I recognised the sweet tones as they drew nearer to me, and instantly felt differently. Overwhelmed, excited, but hesitant, like I did on the beach that time, when I'd returned from my aunt's. Helena was here in front of me! She stopped abruptly, and I smiled. The flowers she was holding now fell to her side.

"You OK? You look as though you've seen a ghost!" Rob asked her.

"I'm fine," she reassured him, but her attention was on me. Her only expression was of disbelief. And I could sense this feeling as not being warm and welcoming like all our other encounters. This was very different. I stayed where I was as they moved closer. Rob took the seat next to Jamie as he slept. Helena whispered to Rob not to wake him.

"I'm going to put these in water, OK?" she whispered, and gestured for me to follow.

She walked back through the long corridor, passing the other departments, as I followed silently behind. I sensed she was uptight. And then she turned towards me at the end of the corridor.

"Gabriel, what are you doing here?"

I smiled. I'd missed her!

"I wanted to surprise you. It's been ages. I knew you were busy, so I thought I would come and support you."

"You certainly surprised me all right, but I told you I would contact you soon. After all it wasn't that long ago. Yesterday, in fact."

I smiled. I couldn't help it. I could sense she was angry but I didn't care.

"Like I said, ages ago. I know what you said, but I needed to see you!"

Her tension softened slightly.

"I was waiting for you to call but you didn't, so here I am."

The softening of the tension didn't last long, though. I could feel the air of discomfort she had for being there with me then.

"How did you know how to find me?"

"Your father. I called. He told me you would be here. Said you stayed at Rob's house. You didn't say."

I could really sense she was not happy now.

"Look, Gabriel! Go home. I'll call at yours later, when I'm finished here, OK?"

I just couldn't understand where all this unhappiness within her was coming from. There was no reason for it. I smiled, trying to keep the situation as calm as possible. She didn't need any fuel from me to keep this anger going.

"Right! I'm going back," she said as she turned and walked away.

There was no room for any further conversation. I watched her walk away.

My head was full of emotions right then, mainly hers I think.

All of this was weighty, painful and really confusing. Clearly something wasn't right. If only she'd say what was going on in her mind. I was helpless not knowing, and the feeling that stayed with me was so painful.

Was this what friends were meant to feel?

16

Sense of Being

Helena didn't call me before she came. She'd left me wondering all evening. In fact it was getting quite late, so I'd convinced myself she wouldn't turn up, not tonight at least. Her mood seemed softer this time as she entered the house. I was a little confused to how to approach her this evening, especially if the encounter earlier in the day was anything to go by. I wanted to give her my usual winning smile on her arrival but held back. It hadn't gone down so well the last couple of times.

"Hi," I said as I invited her in.

I showed her through to the sitting room. She was silent. In fact she looked drawn and tired – hardly surprising really.

"Would you like something to drink?" I asked.

"Yes. Water would be great, thanks."

I couldn't feel any emotions from her. Very different from earlier.

"How is Jamie doing?" I asked as I walked back from the kitchen.

"He's doing a lot better now that they've got his pain relief under control."

It was strange talking like this. I could feel a barrier between us, as though all our previous closeness was nowhere to be seen.

"And you, how are you doing?" I was conscious of how I was conducting this conversation, with poise and maturity. The previous excitement and child-like play was not the best tactic.

"Yeah, I'm OK. A little tired, but OK. Gabriel, I called tonight because there's something I wanted to talk to you about."

"OK, that sounds bad. Am I in trouble again?" I let out a smirk but wished I hadn't. I realised that the conversation deserved a more mature attitude. "Sorry! You were saying." I tried to reassure her that I understood the situation better now and I was giving it my full attention. I was also feeling a little nervous, unsure of the situation, of what was to come. I couldn't read her. Her emotions were not predictable, not laid bare for me to read. She was calm and collected, her responses thought through.

"I've had something on my mind and I need to talk to you about it."

"OK." I was really intrigued.

"It's something that's been really puzzling me."

"I knew something was wrong. Is this why you've been so different?" I asked.

"Yes. I'm sorry about that. It wasn't my intention. It's just that there are things that have been said and I'm confused about it…"

I cut her off. "What do you mean, things that have been said? I don't understand."

"Well, it's just one thing really that I just can't get my head around." She looked awkward.

"I really don't get what you're trying to say." And then I twigged, jumping to a conclusion, and sprang to the edge of my chair in front of her. My hands opened, as if to offer comfort from afar. She too sat forward. There was clear sadness in her eyes, as she fought to get the words out.

"Look, Helena! They are bound to feel this way about us at first. After all, they've known you a lot longer than I have. It'll be fine. They'll soon come around."

I had begun to feel as anxious as she was. I had no knowledge of people's closeness to each other before, and how changes created other feelings. It was an admirable quality, I thought.

"Gabriel, it's not us. It's you!"

"Me? But why? What do you mean?" I was totally confused. A mixture of emotions came flooding through me. But I could see she was having a hard time in talking about this too. "Helena! Just tell me. It's obviously bothering you, so just say it." I was beginning to hate what all this anxiety was doing to us both, and I wanted to get rid of it.

"OK. Look! You know yesterday when we were going to meet my friends at the diner and Rob turned up?"

I tried to compose myself to recollect the memories of that day. "Yes, of course."

"And I went to speak with him at the door, whilst you stayed put. Remember?"

"Yes." I was really intrigued to know the ending to all these pieces I'd put together in my mind.

"Do you remember us both looking back at you?" Helena asked.

"Yes, that's right."

"Rob told me he wasn't able to stay. He had to get back to the hospital. That day was important to me. I wanted to introduce you to them, but with the accident and all, that moment was gone. They knew they were going to meet you and of course Rob was curious," she rambled on, almost as if she was reliving the event.

"Hels, what are you going on about?"

"Just wait. I'm trying to tell you." She had that puzzled look in her eyes again.

"What?" The intensity of the situation was overwhelming. I wished she'd just say it.

She was silent for a moment. I could sense concern and bewilderment in her eyes.

"I could see you sat there, watching us, but, well…" She paused slightly. "He couldn't…" She was looking at me with pleading eyes.

"He couldn't what? What you on about? What does that mean?" I really didn't know what she was getting at. I tried to think back to that time, to remember where I was situated. If my memory served me right, I was in clear view of them both. There was nothing strange about that.

"He couldn't see you, Gabriel! At first I thought he wasn't looking properly or you weren't in view of him but you were." She still had that pleading look etched on her face.

"But I don't understand. I was there, in front of you. You saw me, didn't you?"

"Yes, Gabriel, I did and there should have been no reason for Rob not to have seen you either, but he didn't. In fact he thought you'd walked off somewhere. I had to agree with him to make it sound less ridiculous as I could quite clearly see you sitting there in front of us."

My mouth was unable to say anything. My mind refused to understand what she was saying and certainly could not make any sense of it.

"I really wasn't sure what to do. What he'd said…" I heard Helena pleading.

"Well, you could have told me this at the time." I realised my attitude was slightly negative and blunt but I couldn't help myself. I had no understanding of what she had just told me. I could not work it out!

"Yeah, you're right. I should have told you straightaway, but like you I was struggling to get my head around it. I'm sorry, Gabriel."

I just sat there. All sorts of stuff whizzed around in my head but none of it made sense. There was also an element of hurt that washed over me now. Hurt, that she had treated me so… so flippantly. Had we not had a bond between us, something special that united us to care for one another's well-being?

"So I guess that's why you've been the way you have with me?"

"I'm so sorry, Gabriel, for the way I've behaved. There is no excuse for it," she explained.

"Hmm."

I kept thinking about the situation in the diner, trying to work out why Rob hadn't seen me. My thoughts turned to the hospital visit. How I was stood there, in front of both of them, when they walked into the ward. He must have seen me then. There was no way he wouldn't. I was the only one in there at the time. I was convinced I had the answer.

"But the hospital visit today? He saw me when you came in."

"No, Gabriel! Sorry, but he didn't." Helena was looking concerned now, but I sensed not for herself. "Look, Gabriel, there must be some rational reason for all of this."

"Oh, yeah! You think?" I said, irritated. I couldn't grasp this stuff. "Look, Helena! I need to get to grips with this. And I would like to be alone right now, so…" This feeling of irritation was really deep within me now. Having her around now was just too much. Having to be polite when really my frustration was at boiling point. I needed her to go, so I could think.

"Gabriel, look, I can stay if you like. I don't mind." She moved closer now. I sensed an air of warmth, compassion, within her now that I had not felt for a while.

"No! No, thank you. I just need my own space right now. Please just go. Go away," I could hear myself saying.

I watched her sadness instantly start to grow in front of me. Sadness, perhaps because I had put it there, I had rejected her. Who was this person? I didn't recognise him. Who had I become? I felt a moment's sadness for myself.

"OK. But call me tomorrow, OK? I need to know you're

alright," she said, walking towards the door, with me following behind.

There were no further words or gestures between us. I'm not sure that there was anything further to say, anyway. I stood in the porch as I watched her drive away. I closed the door behind me, my head hanging low, my brain going over and over what had been said tonight, and none of it making the slightest bit of sense to me.

What was this all about? What did this mean?

How was it that she could see me but he couldn't? Was I some kind of freak? No, there had to be a logical explanation. There just had to be. She could see me, couldn't she? And then I remembered. Her father could also see me and converse with me, as I remembered the several conversations we had shared. What was that all about, then? Her friend must have been mistaken, I was convinced. But it wasn't long before the doubt set in again. Why would he say all of this, if it wasn't true? What reason did he have? None! He had no reason to lie. The whole situation had made me cold, detached from myself; all that I'd known and done, questionable. I thought about that now. Hadn't I'd been different though? I'd known that from the moment I arrived here, that I had a sense of needing to be close to her. Where had that come from? Hadn't I felt that in the station during my first encounter with her? And then when I returned, all that energy that flooded through me, that I hadn't had before, was overpowering. I was able to sense her thoughts, her feelings, her very being. Was that why I was here, somehow? But what did that mean? What did that make me? And if I wasn't me, then who was I? I battled to figure them out, but all my questions remained unanswered.

17

Memories

The night before had come and gone in a blur. As I lay there on the bed, contemplating the things that were discussed, the numbness I felt the night before still remained. I couldn't remember going to bed but somehow I had. Even that was strange, not being able to remember things like that, and it wasn't the first time. In fact there were several situations that had happened without thought, and yet they happened all the same. I tried to piece together what had been said, but in a more calm way than yesterday. I would need to apologise to Helena. My reaction to her comments could have been less aggressive. After all, she was only the messenger. Having the time to digest this on my own allowed me to think logically. If what Helena had said was true, then how was it that she was able to see me?

And how, for that matter, was it that her father was able to see me too? It didn't make much sense to me. However, some things were strange even to me. Sitting on the edge of the bed now, my head in my hands, I thought of what brought me here, to this house. Yes, my father in a way pushed me into making a move from my aunt's, to enable me to be more independent, but he never suggested coming here, to this house. Where had that idea come from? I had no memory of that. And yet coming here, as far as I could remember, was where I truly felt I belonged. I never had that before but here everything was different. I had sensed the changes from the moment I arrived – the evening in the station, the night Helena was there. I never knew her before, and yet when I saw her waiting there for the situation to end, I was instantly drawn to her. It was as though it was meant to be, my being there at that moment, but how was that possible? I couldn't recall how I got there and even why I was there in the first place. This was the first thing that didn't make sense. And then there was the time at the picture house, a very similar situation to the one with Rob at the diner. And the time her workmate looked over at me and I watched Helena's face. At the time I didn't take too much notice, but I remembered now she had that sort of confused look on her face. She didn't say a thing at the time so I let it go, but thinking about it now made me look at it in a different light. Could it be that she had not seen me either? The waitress in the diner afterwards had placed the meals on the table without reference to me. Was it that she hadn't seen me either? All these things were beginning to mount up and, yes, though I didn't want to admit it, there was something not quite right about all of this. I wondered now whether or not I had ever had any personal contact with another person. I had no recollection of it. But if this was so, then why? Why me? For what reason? Who was able to give me any answers? My head was buzzing with so much confusion. I needed to know.

Feeling exhausted, I lay back down again. It felt never-ending, this stuff going over and over, round and round. I hated this, all this crap. I just wanted it all to go away, for it to be normal again, for me to be normal again, but the truth was, I wasn't normal, not like everyone else. So where did I fit? The life I'd chosen for myself here was not real; it was an illusion, a fake, just like me. I could feel the swell of anger stirring inside me. Everything I had come to know had all been a lie – a home, a life, a love. My body wilted at the thought of her, Helena. I had learnt so much about myself, my emotions, all since she had been in my life. But how could I carry on this way? How could she? Answers were needed, but where from?

The sound of the cellphone beside me woke me with a start. It was Helena. I quickly grappled with the front flap of the phone in order to answer her.

"Hello, Helena. Are you OK?"

"Yes, I'm fine. You?"

I wanted to say, I'm feeling terrible, lost, confused, in limbo. Had no sense of who I was? But I didn't. It would serve no purpose to be self-loathing in front of her.

"Yeah, I'm OK."

"I was thinking. How about you come down to the house? Maybe we could go for a walk or something," Helena said.

The very thought of that filled me with dread. I wanted to be nowhere near anybody. I was a freak in my own home. It was hard enough thinking, let alone dealing with all of this in front of other folk.

"Do you mind if we change the venue? Perhaps you could come here instead?"

"Yeah. Why not." She hesitated for a moment. "See ya in a while, OK?" She had such a soothing nature, especially when she spoke.

"Yep!"

I couldn't wait to see her. Watching her go last night I was in a different frame of mind. Emotions were running overtime, all of which I had not experienced before. I felt claustrophobic the previous night, unable to breath. So although in normal circumstances I would not have wanted her to go, it was what I needed to get through it.

I sensed her walk towards the door, as I made my way there myself, although I thought that she had got here very quickly. As

I opened the door I was not ready for what was now facing me. The light was so bright; blinding, in fact. I averted my eyes as I clung onto the door frame with one hand, shielding my eyes with the other.

"Wow! What is that?"

I could sense pressure from within the light but no one spoke.

"Hey, is anyone there?"

There was still no answer. This light was so bright, it was really hurting my eyes. It was hard to keep them open.

"What is this? Look, is there anyone there?"

Again, nothing. I was reluctant to walk any further forward, a little unsure as to what I might find.

"Helena? Is that you?"

There was a pause before the sweetest voice answered.

"No, Gabriel."

I was a little taken aback. Although I wanted a response, I wasn't expecting to get one.

"Who are you?"

Again, another pause.

"Someone that loves you," the voice replied.

"This is crazy! Show yourself!" All this uncertainty was driving me mad.

"Gabriel! Search yourself, as I come to you now, who am I?" the voice said softly.

I searched but there was nothing. But wait. There, deep down, stored away, was the nicest memory, one I had preserved for so long that I had forgotten it was even there. It was a memory I had from when I was a small boy. I thought very carefully, trying to get it right. I remembered the sweetness of the voice. Was it the same voice? Could it be?

"My mother?" It came out as a question because although my

memory pointed me in this direction, logic told me I had to be wrong. It was a mistake, had to be. She was dead!

Moments later I found I was able to remove my hand from my eyes. The light was dimming, becoming bearable. As I re-focused them, there stood in front of me a figure, a beautiful figure of a woman. She was dressed in a long, flowing white gown that touched the floor. It flowed as if there was a slight breeze blowing it that way. Her black hair tumbled around her shoulders, framing her face. Her whole presence was shrouded in a soft dimming light that only centred on her. The whole vision was stunning and unexplained, yet it now stood in front of me. Logically I should have been shocked or something, but I wasn't. There weren't any of those feelings within me. I was totally calm.

"Yes, Gabriel!" she said with a soft smile.

I knew this was the truth; my feelings told me so. And my memories now also told me that this had not been the first time I had seen her.

"You have searched your inner self, Gabriel, and know it to be true. I am here now because you have need of me. You have finally become a man and with that responsibility comes great changes. I am here now, Gabriel, to help you. But for me to do this, you must learn to let go of everything you have known before and freely open your mind to encompass other things."

My mouth was open but I could not say a word. I just stood there. I was at ease but confused. How was it that she was dead and yet here? Was this my imagination playing tricks with me? This wasn't possible! Maybe I was still upstairs asleep and dreaming all this. It was just so confusing!

"Gabriel? You are here. This is not a dream. I know you are struggling with this but the answers are coming. Be patient, my son!" she said so reassuringly.

There! How did she know all that stuff? Things I had just thought of!

"We are the same, you and I. And soon all will become clear."

What did that mean? "We are the same." I was the same as what? My mother? Dead? It was all so frustrating. What was going on here? What was it that I needed to know? Why couldn't I know now? I could feel myself getting agitated, anxious.

"Be patient, my son," she repeated, her smile so sweet to reassure me, I guess.

I was aware the light inside the front door had become brighter again. My instant reaction, to cover my eyes again, was stopped in mid-flow. It was not needed. The light was moving outwards, surrounding me now. But I wasn't frightened at all. In fact, it seemed to calm the previous feelings of anguish. I was in awe of it, as we were now both encased in it. It was a strange feeling. A kind of physical being still remained but without the heaviness. All my previous unrest seemed reduced somehow. She held out her hand as if for me to take it.

"Ready, Gabriel?"

Ready for what? I thought. But even with that in mind, I felt this was right now, being here in this way.

"Yes."

She smiled and took my hand, as my most recent thoughts left me there, waiting, looking for her, as her image passed through my mind. I had forgotten her, but she was here now, waiting for me.

Helena.

And I drifted.

Book Three

Helena

18

Reunion

He seemed different this morning, much calmer. It was understandable for him to be angry with me last night. I'd been sitting on this stuff, acting like a selfish bitch, when I should have been sharing this with him a lot sooner. After all, it was about him. Didn't he have a right to know? I don't know what I was thinking. If it had been me getting this news, I'm sure I would have acted the same way. I so hoped he would forgive me for my actions, and that I could make up for my wrongdoing somehow. I wasn't sure how. After all, I didn't understand the implications of what I had told him, but I hoped between us we could come up with some answers.

"Yeah. Why not?" I paused for a moment, as I listened for his reply over the phone.

What was going through his mind? Had I said something wrong? It was clear he was still struggling with this. I thought for a moment. Of course, how stupid was I? How could I have not thought this through? Why would he want to come down here, go for a walk and be around people? That was like rubbing salt in the wound. One moment I am telling him that people can't see him, that he is somehow invisible to others, and the next I'm asking him to carry on as normal. But how can it be normal for him now? Asking me instead to go to his house, would make perfect sense. How could I be so thoughtless, again!

"See ya in a while, OK?" I replied.

121

I felt so bad as I closed the shutter on my cell, disconnecting the call between us. How could I have not thought before I'd opened my big mouth? I couldn't believe I had done it again.

Gabriel didn't deserve this. He was such a kind and gentle person. He had showed me nothing else. I grabbed my stuff, said my farewells to Dad, and headed out to the car. Dad had given me more access to his car of late with Jamie in hospital and all. It was easier than waiting for a bus.

As I climbed into the seat, my mind was still troubled by my stupidity in all of this. But to be fair I was still struggling with it myself. I was trying to understand how it was possible that my Dad and I were able to see him but others couldn't. It just didn't make any sense.

Driving through the lane towards the house I was aware of how wet the road was this morning and how foggy it had become all of a sudden. A blanket had covered the whole area, making visibility really poor.

By the time I'd reached the top of the hill and levelled out towards the house, the fog had disappeared and brilliant sunshine greeted me instead. I smiled. The sun had that effect on me. It made me feel warm and happy somehow. I had to admit, as I was getting closer, my stomach felt nervous, churned up. I know I'd spoken with him already this morning but I was able to hide my vulnerability then. However, whenever he was in my presence he had a canny knack of knowing how I was feeling. That in itself had a strange feel to it. Did that have any significance to what I had told him yesterday? The thought washed away from me as I pulled up to the house. I noted the immediate smells coming from the garden, and how well it was kept. I presumed it had a natural way of preserving itself, as I'd never noticed anyone tending it before. As I crossed the ground towards the house, I noticed the front door was wide open. Perhaps he was busy and left it that way for me to just walk in.

"Gabriel?" I cried out, walking in.

I stood in the porch, waiting for him to call out in acknowledgement.

"Gabriel? It's Helena," I said as I closed the door behind me.

The house was unusually quiet. I took a few steps into the house, and walked towards the foot of the staircase. Maybe he was upstairs.

"Gabriel, you up there?"

I glanced around the house. Everything was perfectly placed. Where on earth was he? He knew I was coming; it was his suggestion. A thought entered my head. Maybe he was outside. After all, the front door was wide open when I arrived. I took a look outside. Nothing. It was really strange. Where was he?

"Gabriel? It's Helena," I repeated, hoping he'd pop around from the corner of the house. But there was nothing. I turned and walked back into the house, looking around as I went, hoping to see something that would give me a clue as to where he could be. Maybe he had gone out, but then that just didn't make sense. He knew I was coming so why would he. And the door was open; anyone could have walked in. It just didn't make sense. I'll phone him, I thought, as I grabbed my cell from my pocket. I listened for a connection. The tone rang as I placed it to my ear. I could hear the faint shrill of another ringing, as I looked for the connection. The noise was coming from upstairs. I entered each room, looking for his phone, as I left mine still ringing downstairs. Finally I found the ringing phone on the bedside cabinet. But he was nowhere to be seen. I sat on the edge of the bed as I tried to make sense of this. I checked the wardrobe and the chest of drawers for any sign that he had taken off, maybe. But no, everything seemed intact. So where was he?

I scribbled a note and left it on the downstairs table. He wouldn't miss it there when he got back. I couldn't help thinking that the whole thing was just too weird. There could only be one logical explanation – he had to have gone out, but leaving the door open like that and his cell upstairs suggested he left in a hurry. Thinking about it as I closed the door behind me and made for the car, a similar thing had happened before, when I met his father here. Maybe that was it!

Had he gone to his aunt's again? Something must be wrong. That makes sense. That must be it! Sitting in the car, mulling this all over in my head, I decided I was happy to accept my last thought as the explanation. It made sense. My nervousness was now replaced by disappointment. As I drove away, taking a second look at the house, I hoped I had missed something and that he would pop his head from around the corner and surprise me. But of course, he didn't.

19

Graduation

The next couple of weeks were taken up by regular visits to see Jamie in the hospital. His injuries were on the mend and he was desperate to escape. He made it obvious he was bored senseless. But Rob did his best to keep his spirits high. So although my mind was occupied with the whereabouts of Gabriel, my time was solely taken up by other things going on around me. I hadn't heard a word from Gabriel in nearly three weeks. I was mostly satisfied with my reasoning that he had taken off to his aunt's again, especially with the way I'd found things at the house that day, but still a couple of things didn't add up. Surely he would have taken clothes with him, but surprisingly all were intact. Helena had known from her previous visits that Gabriel's wardrobe was very limited. It seemed nothing had gone, as if he hadn't actually gone anywhere. He hadn't tried to contact me. I expected him to have done that at least, if only to make up for the previous time it happened.

So a few things didn't quite add up. But there was no one who knew him to ask.

Time passed; in fact until it was actually nearly two months since I last spoke to Gabriel. Things had carried on much as before. Jamie had made a really good recovery from his injuries, although he'd be left with some scars for a while. Rob was back to his old self now he had his sidekick back by his side again. Sometimes it was difficult to watch how Rob seemed a shadow form of himself without Jamie around. He almost seemed lost, fragile maybe; not a sight I was used to seeing.

Work was the same old thing and college was winding up in another three weeks for the summer break. But those weeks would be packed to the brim with finishing final assignments to get in on time. Stressful times! This was it, what the last three years were all about, and now it was all coming to an end. Secretly I felt great excitement about graduating but it wasn't just about that. It also said I had grown up and was qualified to get a job I wanted. It would be easier to find one, especially when there were very few jobs and thousands looking at the same one. But I would have the qualification, so did I have the upper hand? Well, that's what they told us at school. However, thinking about work was scary stuff. I guess that's why I hadn't even let it cross my mind. I knew it was there in the back of my mind but it wasn't stressing me out; it was just a niggle. I was just playing with the idea of being an adult. My job at the cinema was really like earning pocket money. It hadn't given me that bigger responsibility yet. That would come later and I guessed that was where the scary part would come in. Socialising with the boys – well, I say the boys; I really mean only Rob, as Jamie had only recently been discharged from the hospital – had pretty much gone out of the window of late. Spare time was spent in my room, trying to pull pieces of art work together, ready for the rapidly approaching deadline. The only socialising I actually did these days was on the Internet.

When it was quiet in the house, my mind would wander, thinking about Gabriel and what he was up to. There was still no contact from him, and several times I thought about visiting the house, like I had before, in the hope that I'd be surprised when I got there, but thought better of it. I was sure that if he was back he would come to see me. And I desperately needed to believe that, especially if his feelings towards me were the same as mine for him. I missed so much about him, like that smile when he was trying to reassure me things would be OK, and his gentlemanly manner, dancing with my emotions, showing me so much more to love. I remembered that at first it was me who had talked about my feelings openly, but gradually he had joined in and after a while it was as though we had so much to talk about. There just wasn't enough time to say it all. And he loved listening to me talk about how things were when I was a child, and the places we went to as a family. He spoke about his family, mainly about his aunt and the places they would go together; mainly local, but it sounded so adventurous. He hardly mentioned his father and when his name cropped up unexpectedly he would quickly change the subject. It was so apparent that there was no love lost between them. But his aunt; the love he had for her was impossible to express. She was everything to him. So it wasn't surprising now that he would want to do everything he possibly could for her, but it didn't stop me missing him.

I managed to cut my hours right down at the cinema over the following weeks, to allow me time for the assignments that needed my attention. I was surprised at how much work and determination I'd already put into getting them finished, and I thought it was beginning to rub off on the guys. My Facebook page was alive with queries and answers, back and forth. A break away after completing this little lot was definitely on the cards. Rob had sorted out a night out for us all to celebrate once we finished. Yes, it was a great idea but not really my kind of thing, but I agreed to go unwillingly, not least because they thought it good to tell my dad, who thought it was a great idea of course. They knew their ally well! Of course, he was right as usual. But I wished Gabriel was there. I wanted to celebrate this time with him, somewhere quiet with a place to talk about my next step in life. Because from here on, the next week or so was the end of one thing and the beginning of something else. He was good at that stuff, reassuring me that things would work out and right now that was what I needed. A significant part of me was frightened of what lay ahead and without him by my side I was exposed to this powerful feeling. I felt a lump in my throat as my memories of him took hold. The pain subsided from my eyes as I fought back the tears that welled up, ready to flow.

Finally, graduation day was here! I had waited so long for this day. I'm not sure why but I had; we all had. Reluctantly I bought the gown and cap for the ceremony at my Dad's persistence. I would have been quite happy in my jeans but Dad wouldn't hear of it. Rob and Jamie's excitement was at fever pitch, and had been for weeks building up to this. But I wasn't sure whether it was the ceremony or the party afterwards that was fuelling their quite obvious zeal. Jamie had found out that his mum, along with other parents, had organised a celebratory party for us. Of course he was sworn to secrecy, but Jamie wasn't that good in keeping his end of the bargain, so now everyone knew. Graduation was also their moment, a time for the proud parents to watch, smiles beaming. We were their little boys and girls, all grown up. And they would savour the moment for a lifetime, through many pictures that would be taken this day.

Sitting, waiting for my name to be called to collect my diploma, my mind wandered. A part of me had hoped that he'd surprise me and be waiting for me when we arrived. Dad, I think, had noticed that disappointment as he grabbed my hand and shot me a reassuring smile. The guys were still very hyper. They'd been like it all day. If I didn't know better, I'd think they were on some sort of drug. Both sets of parents were there for Rob and Jamie, which was so cool. However, I wasn't so sure in how Rob was dealing with that. He wasn't exactly close with his stepdad but it pleased his Mum. Jamie, on the other hand, had a different kind of relationship with his stepmother. She understood the importance of keeping the relationship between him and his father intact. When it was my turn to walk on stage, I wanted to die with the embarrassment of it all. I could hear the loud applause from my proud father but more than that, I heard the guys chanting and wolf-whistling through the crowd. Thank goodness I only had to go up the once!

After the ceremony we all split up and went our separate ways. Dad had arranged to take me out for a meal. It was a chance to catch up. We hadn't done too much of that lately, especially with me stuck up in my room swotting away on assignments. It was also a moment for Dad to talk about Mum and how she would have enjoyed all of this, how proud she would have been seeing her little girl collecting her prize. It was quite a sentimental mealtime but I understood and appreciated it. Dad was right. Mum would have been in her element. We watched each other from across the table as memories flooded back, and we smiled at each other in acknowledgement that we had both realised this.

The day had come and gone in a blink, I reflected. Rob had left me several texts, giving me the lowdown on his afternoon. He sounded like he was bored, going on about tonight's party, which I would rather have forgotten. I was exhausted lying in my room trying to relax, but my mind was too occupied by the day's events, and something else. Him! I was so sure that Gabriel would come to see me. Today of all days. He knew how I felt about today. We'd talked so many times about it and he assured me he'd be there for me. Disappointment swelled within me as the hot stinging of tears trickled down my cheeks. It had been months and no word. Surely! Feelings of loneliness and abandonment increased. Stop!

Stop this! I was determined not to do this, to think like this. No! I told myself I needed to be strong and get on with it. Gabriel would be here when he was able and that was that. I just hoped it wouldn't be too much longer.

20

Dream State

The cold, dark night surrounded me as I walked through the dense woodland. There was a feeling of frozen time, as if everything was going on around me, but not to me. There were sounds of plants breathing and critters scurrying around in the undergrowth, and I was in tune with the noises. The ground was still wet underfoot from some rainfall. As I looked down I saw that the leaves were all soggy. It was just like winter. Water droplets fell from the branches above me as I searched in the moonlit night. The scene was alive! I could feel my body move forward through the thick woodland but was not aware of my limbs moving. It was a weird sensation! There was no need to look closely at where I was walking; my body needed no guidance. It was drifting slowly forward of its own free will.

The trees on either side seemed to move in closer towards me, like they were trying to enclose me. There were no smells either, just the echoing silences. It could only be described as being in a bubble. I was now aware of an image standing in the distance as I moved towards it. I had no feelings of despair or panic. I felt perfectly calm.

As I drew closer, a sense of knowing, of remembering, washed over me. I was unable to make out the figure that was there, but as the momentum seemed to take me faster, the feelings within me grew stronger. I could feel this presence all around me, as if it was inside my very soul. It reminded me of the time on the beach. I felt a longing to be close. He was here now, in front of me, waiting. I called his name over and over but the bubble effect seemed to keep the words enclosed within it. He could not hear me. Panic crept over me and I felt his unhappiness as he turned away from me. I tried so desperately to move my legs faster, but I sensed a feeling of defeat within me as I knew they weren't moving.

They felt heavy and fatigued. I willed my stride to stretch further, hoping that I would finally catch up with him as he walked away. I summoned all my strength and energy and pushed myself forward as I lunged out my hand to catch his forearm.

"Gotcha!"

I was totally exhausted. I could hear my heavy breathing in my ear.

"Gabriel?" My voice was heavy, my breathing trying to regain itself.

It was strange saying anything because it felt like it could only be heard in here. His smell was so beautiful. It was a strange thought but it was the only smell that I could identify. He was wearing another one of his pristine suits. He looked so dashing in it! He turned. I was not prepared for what was now facing me. I was confused and I'm sure it must have shown. The bright shimmer that surrounded his face took me aback at first, and I strained to see his features through it.

"Gabriel."

I was taken back because what emerged through the light was a face I had not expected to see, but one I knew. My facial expression must have betrayed my confusion. I was convinced it had been him; everything told me that. But instead it was his father who stood here before me now, staring at me, straight-faced, no emotions showing. He uttered not one word of acknowledgement or any pleasantries; nothing. He just stood there, silent. It was really eerie. The bright light still remained around him as he stood there. I hadn't really noticed that before when I first met him. I was used to seeing Gabriel in this light; somehow it was part of who he was.

I accepted it without thought. My hand released his arm as I watched him turn back to walk away. It was strange he hadn't said a word to me. Surely he remembered me?

"Mr King, please don't go. Gabriel, do you know where he is?"

The walls of trees seemed to move in closer, as if they were caving in around us, as the distance between us became greater. I wanted to move forward, chase after him, but my will could not push the bubble forward. I could only watch in frustration at being encased in this thing, this entity.

"Mr King, please?" I screamed after him.

I watched as he suddenly turned in the distance. He was too far ahead for me to really see him, just a shadowy image in the darkness, a silhouette of the man who had stood before me. The trees were still moving in to enclose us. I was beginning to feel frightened, trapped in this bubble. I couldn't move. They were going to crush me. The darkness was everywhere. The trees started to blow around, gently at first and then more violently.

Branches threw themselves around harder and harder until they were touching the ground with each swish. I watched as they uprooted themselves with force and flew around my head like a hurricane. I watched in amazement. Fear gripped me tight. I was rigid.

There was no sound, just pictures, as if I was in some sort of non-speaking film. I could feel the damp prickly wetness on my palms. In fact I was aware my whole body felt this way.

Gabriel's father still stood there in the distance whilst all of this was going on around us.

I watched as a light shone brightly around me. I looked around for its source. I could hear a faint voice coming from somewhere. Again I looked. The light was the only thing I could see now. The scene of swirling trees had now gone; only the light remained. I strained to hear the voice that was there now but could not quite catch what it said. The voice was sweet, female-sounding; endearing, in fact. My fear had passed, the uncomfortable feelings of dampness over my body were all but gone. I was beginning to feel more relaxed.

"He will ask you," a faint, sweet voice said.

My mind was *buzzing*, questioning, searching the light for something, anything that would explain this.

"What will he ask? Who?" I asked in reply.

But there was nothing.

"Who?" I asked again, looking around for a sign, any sign that would answer any of this.

There was nothing. The light had gone. Blackness remained and nothing else. I could feel myself drifting down slowly, like floating. There was an instant feeling of being free, weightless. But the feeling didn't last long. It changed as quickly as it had begun. I felt frightened again. The falling sensation was faster this time and I was powerless to stop it. I felt panic seize me and I hated how that felt. All my emotions wanted to scream out, cry, anything to make this stop. But my voice was empty; it wouldn't work. I just couldn't get my words out. My voice broke as I pleaded for the only person I wanted now. Gabriel, please, I heard myself say, as I felt my whole body just let go and drift into the darkness. I was conscious of the smell that now surrounded me, the smell I had come to know so well, the familiarity of his face upon mine. The embrace I had known before. I opened my eyes, as a familiar smile greeted me. Without thought, mine was there to greet him also. I was aware my body was laid out flat but the softness of the space below me wasn't the ground. It was weightless and so was I. My surroundings were so bright; not bright light as such, rather white and fluffy instead. I felt so safe here. I watched his face as I stared up at him now and he caught my stare. He had a beautiful face, so angelic, warm and protective.

"Gabriel, where?" I felt my voice say. However I didn't remember actually opening my mouth.

He smiled again so reassuringly, as he had done so many times before.

"Soon Helena, soon!" The sound of his voice drifted over to me.

I smiled back, my eyes feeling heavy. They fought to stay open, to keep the last images of him with me.

"It's OK, sleep now," he reassured me, as my eyes gave in and my lids closed together.

My eyes darted to the alarm clock that was screaming at me now. They were still heavy with sleepiness. I reached over and switched it off, taking a quick glance at the time. I lay back down on the bed as before, my mind still *buzzing* with fragments of the dream I had just woken from. There were pieces of the dream that still remained but I could not recollect the whole story. I still felt the warmth of his embrace as he engulfed all of me, the strength of his smile and – oh, God! – his smell. I was so helpless around him in these moments. I smiled at the lasting memory he had left me.

21

A Celebration

"Helena, you ready yet?" Dad called up to me.

We were going together to the celebrations tonight. I was nearly ready. I hadn't realised just how tired I was. The graduation ceremony had really taken its toll. The nervous energy that built in me during the day had reached a point where sleep was a necessity. There was no piece left of the dream, no shards of any reminder of what was involved.

"Nearly," I shouted back in reply.

I took a long look at myself in the bedroom mirror. The dress actually didn't look too bad on me, I mused. Although I thought the heels on my shoes wouldn't last too long, especially with my clumsy feet in them. A lady I was not. I liked comfort too much. I grabbed my stuff from the bed and made my way downstairs.

"I'm ready," I said as I searched for Dad in the house. "Dad?"

"Baby, I'm here."

I found him in the conservatory, only it wasn't just him there. I was confronted by a figure I hadn't expected and I think my open-mouthed expression said it all. I was speechless. I just stood there, unable to say anything.

"Well, aren't you going to say anything?" my Dad piped up.

I was still in shock, mesmerised by him as he sat there.

"Yeah, yeah, course," I reassured him.

"Gabriel has just got back and wanted to escort you to tonight's party," Dad said, trying to continue the conversation.

"Really, but what about you?" I asked. I relaxed more. The shock was wearing off slightly.

"If that's OK with you?" His voice sounded so velvety smooth. Different somehow, more grown up.

"No, I'll come along anyway and stay for a while. I was only going to hang around for a short time anyway. You know how that boom-boom music irritates me," Dad explained. "Hey, you look nice! So the dress fitted you, then?" he said, as he spied me up and down.

My face felt instant heat as I bowed my head. I was embarrassed! "Thanks, Dad!"

I watched as Gabriel looked at me with his deep, meaningful expression. He smiled. "Yes, you are beautiful, Helena!" he said.

By now my face was on fire. Why did he have to say that in that way? His voice sounded so tender and warm but in the same breath I sensed something else, rather more sensual and mean-ingful. It was as though his words had something more to say. I looked up and stared deep into his dark eyes, as I felt them draw me in, lifting me into a weightless dream state.

"Thanks!" I acknowledged, blinking.

"You're welcome!" he replied.

I felt so nervous, as if this was the first time I had ever met him. Like a first date. All those overwhelming feelings were with me now as they once were. Strong wrenching sensations in my chest, my stomach doing somersaults. Although I recognised the exterior of the person who stood before me I had no sense of familiarity with the inner person. It was strange. It was as though we had no history between us and we were starting all over again.

Gabriel left his car parked in the drive, Dad taking us in his car. I took in a deep breath of British Summer Time. I really loved this time of year. Warmth still remained from the day. I wore the dress that Dad had picked out for me about a month before. He said he wanted to help me get it, as it would have been something Mum would have done. I understood where he was coming from but was a bit nervous at first with the thought of Dad helping me pick out a garment. But in the end I decided I wasn't exactly a fashion expert myself, so maybe between the two of us we could come up with something at least half decent. To be honest even though I hated clothes shopping, I really enjoyed the time spent with him and seeing the dress on. The results didn't seem too bad at all. Gabriel was wearing one of his gorgeous suits, very formal but in an erotic way somehow. His sense of dress had not revealed this aspect before. It had that Italian feel to it; really cool-looking, begging you to touch. The car was engulfed with his scent, pushing me to take deeper breaths of him. The conversation was confined to Dad going on about work issues, with Gabriel very graciously involving himself. I just sat patiently waiting until I also got the chance to converse with Gabriel but on a more question-and-answer level. I was eager to know what had happened since our last encounter. What had called him away in such a hurry? But that got me thinking about something else. How was he going to do this? After all he couldn't be seen, well, not by Rob in any case. And if he couldn't see Gabriel, then maybe the others couldn't either. That would make things really tricky. Had he forgotten the upset he had endured previously? My having to tell him? We could see him; I mean me and Dad, but it was clear others couldn't. And how should I deal with that? What should I say? Should I act as if he's there with me when we go in or not? I needed to know how he wanted to play this.

"Dad, why don't you go on in? We'll join you in a minute. I need to talk with Gabriel a minute," I said as Dad parked the car.

"OK." And he was gone.

"Is everything OK, Helena?" Gabriel asked, sounding a little curious.

"Well, I'm surprised really," I said looking at him, whilst we both took a seat on a nearby bench.

"What do you mean? Have I done something wrong?" he asked.

He looked really confused. As if he didn't have a clue at what I was getting at.

"No, course not but…" I stopped as I watched people amble past us, girls screaming with excitement, boys trying to look cool, chilling out before they joined the hunt.

It was getting busy. The music indicated that the party had started. Half the guests I didn't even know. I was glad it was a joint party. Dad asked me to put a list together for the invitations, and I could only think of a handful of people.

"What?" Gabriel asked, looking with curiosity at the people arriving.

I was a bit confused myself. From his expression he seemed not to be grasping what I was trying to say. Was it possible he had forgotten? He must have had one hell of a time at his aunt's if that was the case.

"I'm just going to say it then! People! Before you didn't want to be around them and now, well?" I tried to jog his memory.

I could sense he was thinking, searching for something.

"I didn't?" he asked, a puzzled look etched on his face.

This was weird!

"Yes, don't you remember?" I said, watching him physically search his memories now. I wasn't sure about repeating myself. It hadn't gone down so well before, so I was braced for his reaction. "The last time we saw each other. I came to your house. I told you that Rob had not been able to see you." I waited for some kind of a response but there was none. "I apologised for my behaviour at the time but I was confused by it all. You were upset, understandably, and told me you wanted some time alone, and so we arranged to meet the next day at your house, but when I got there I couldn't find you. That was months ago and I haven't heard from you since."

I watched as his eyes darted from place to place. I was dumbfounded by his behaviour. It was as if he didn't have a clue what I was talking to him about. He didn't say a word in response to anything I told him. I guessed from his facial expressions that he wasn't quite ready to sort out what was clearly occupying his mind.

"Gabriel, you look as if you haven't got a clue about anything I've said."

He finally looked up at me but his facial expression hadn't changed.

"You don't, do you?" I said, his expression clearly showing me the answer.

"No?" he said, looking at me as if to say, "I know I should but somehow I don't. But why don't I?"

He looked disgruntled, dishevelled, uneasy with himself. I extended my hand to touch his, hoping to reassure him. He looked and I smiled. His mood and expression instantly changed. Now there was a more confident stance about him, as if the previous few minutes hadn't happened. He returned the smile, which made me a little nervous at first, but then I began to sense something within him that I hadn't before. We had been quite good in the past at sensing each other's feelings but tonight had been strange. I had no sense of him at all, as if he was a stranger of sorts. But now, well, I was beginning to see something familiar in him, the aura around him I knew before. Perhaps he was remembering?

"Gabriel, is something wrong? You OK?"

He cupped my face in his hands and smiled. Wow! I hadn't felt that in a long time. He was coming back to me.

"I am now," he said, studying my face.

"Did I just miss something? I really don't understand. Did

something just happen to you?" I asked.

He had that glow again, that I had for so long taken for granted. But seeing it now made me appreciate it all the more. He was beautiful! Breathtakingly so! I felt a tightness in my chest as I admired him. The emotional tie was still very much there for me.

"Would it sound strange if I said I remembered the importance of something I needed to remember but was not sure what? I know I should but it's as though I'm missing parts of me somehow. There's a lot I need to talk with you about and here is not the right place."

He was still studying me.

"Yeah, you're right. There's things I want to ask you myself."

The warmth of his face staring at mine, made me feel excited, like there was a yearning inside me, desperately wanting to escape, a yearning to throw my arms around him. I'd missed him so much and now at long last he was here, with me. My heart was beating so fast I could hear it in my ears. I wanted him to hold me in his arms as he had before. The commotion of people coming and going around us was of no importance. All I wanted was for him to know how I felt right now. How my heart was beating for him and how I was so glad he had come back to me now. Today of all days, my graduation. How special was that!

He kissed my face very gently. It was so light, that if I hadn't seen him do it, I wouldn't have known, apart from his divine smell that lingered so sweetly around me.

"Helena, I know. I feel it too!" he said, as he smiled again and his eyes met mine.

The moment lingered, as our faces touched and stayed embraced in that moment, his hands cradling my face. I closed my eyes as he held me there, mesmerised by his aura, his sweet, sweet smell and the beat of his precious heart. I rode that feeling, as I drifted sky high into oblivion.

22

The Return

The decision to meet up later after the party was made pretty swiftly.

I did not want to prolong Gabriel's discomfort, if he had any in the first place. However, he was less anxious than expected about being around my mates. But knowing Dad could see him and others couldn't would have made it really difficult for Gabriel to have escorted me in.

We needed to get things sorted out for ourselves first. There were plenty of questions I wanted to ask Gabriel, and he needed to speak with me. I knew Dad wouldn't stay long anyhow, loud music and all that. I would make my excuses to get away then. I guess the guys would be disappointed but they'd soon get over it. They had all their mates and girlfriends there to entertain them, anyhow, and it got me off lightly as I wasn't so keen to be there in the first place. As I walked towards Dad, I could see he was standing with Rob and Jamie and their parents. This would be interesting, trying to explain away Gabriel's departure. Dad had already seen him.

"Hels, where have you been?" Rob asked as he saw me. He rushed towards me and gave me a hug.

"OK, OK, you can let me go now. I'm all squeezed out," I said, and Rob released his grip.

"Where have you been? Your dad was getting worried. You've been ages," he continued as we reached the rest of the group.

"I was just outside talking, that's all."

"Hey, you look great, girl!" Rob said, highlighting me to the group. More embarrassment to deal with. They actually both looked pretty shocked. The guys weren't often given the opportunity to see me all dressed up.

"Yeah, Hels, you look neat," Jamie agreed, with the rest of the group doing the same.

"Hey, Dad!" I said, trying to get his attention over the noise whilst he was talking to Jamie's mother.

"Hi, baby, where you been?" he said as he glanced at me. "Where's Gabriel?" he added, looking around for him.

Here we go. I gotta make it convincing, I thought.

"He had to go home. That's why I was so long. He's not feeling great. He sent his apologies." I could hear myself almost screaming over the top of the music, hopefully coming across believably.

"That's a shame. You should have come and got me. I could have taken him back," he said with a look of real concern creeping across his face.

"It doesn't matter, Dad. He said the walk back would do him some good. He's going to leave his car in our drive, OK?"

"Of course, but it's miles away." I could see Dad thinking about the length of the journey that Gabriel would have.

"He'll be fine, Dad, really! I'll call up later and take his car back." I touched his arm, trying to reassure him.

"OK. I hope you're right."

I sensed that his concern had not completely gone away.

"Is this the famous Gabriel we were supposed to meet a while ago?"

I had not realised that Rob had heard our whole conversation. I had to be cool with my answers, and avoid any unnecessary questions. I tried to make out I hadn't heard him at first but he persisted.

"Hels!" he shouted to get my attention. "That bloke you were talking about; was it the same guy? You know, the one we were supposed to meet months ago. Come on, Hels, think."

I hated lying to the people I loved but it was necessary now. Too many questions otherwise.

"Yeah."

"Where is he then?" He was intrigued, looking around but trying not to look so obvious about it.

The little group we had been in had now dispersed. I saw Jamie taking off with his girlfriend, and Dad had wandered off to chat with others he knew. I was pleased. Hopefully it would be easier to fob off Rob with no spectators.

"He had to go; not well!" I shouted over the noise in the background.

"Right."

Job done! It was easier than I thought. No more questions. It really wasn't like Rob to give up like that. Normally he'd want to know everything, even to the point where he became a pain. Strange that he was not tonight. And that was my cue to start mixing. I mingled with the couple of girls I'd invited from college. We weren't that close but it served as a good distraction.

The evening was a success, so it seemed. Dad and I stayed quite a while. So when we said our goodbyes it wasn't such a big disappointment. It was about ten thirty by the time we got home. Gabriel's car was still in the driveway, just where he left it.

"You know, Hels, that's a long way home for Gabriel. I hope he got back all right," Dad said as he parked next to Gabriel's car.

"Did you speak with him since?" he asked. Seeing the car obviously brought Gabriel to mind again.

"Yeah, he's fine, Dad. The walk home helped, so he said."

I hated lying to Dad. It didn't sit well with me but it served a purpose. I didn't want him fretting over Gabriel. It would make things more complicated.

"Really? Well, that's good," he said, seeming more reassured. "Do you want me to follow you when you take his car back?" he asked, walking into the house.

I was upstairs by now, grabbing things to take with me, whilst still trying to keep the conversation going with him.

"You're alright, Dad. I was thinking I might stay over the night. He's got loads of spare rooms in his house."

I could hear the change in his voice. He was probably surmising what any other parent would.

"Is he OK with this then?" he said as I heard the noise from the TV downstairs.

"Well, I haven't asked him yet but I'm sure he'll be fine about it. Don't worry, Dad. He'll be fine," I said as I went downstairs and headed for the door, not giving him any time to fret over it. I know it would not be easy for him right now letting me go there, his mind probably only coming to one conclusion. "OK, Dad. I'm off. I'll see you tomorrow."

"Yeah. Have a good night. Say hello to Gabriel for me." He tried to sound relaxed, not the overbearing father, but he didn't fool me.

"Love ya."

"Love you too," I heard him say, as I closed the door behind me.

I jumped in the driver's seat, then realised that the car door had been left unlocked and that Gabriel hadn't given me the car keys. I grabbed my bag from the passenger seat to find my cellphone. I listened while the number rang. It was a strange feeling now, after so long, trying to contact him.

"Helena?" I heard him say.

"Yeah, it's me. Hey, I've got no keys to get your car back."

There was silence from the other end.

"Gabriel, did you hear what I said?"

My attention went from the conversation on the cell to some tapping on the driver's window. It was Dad.

"Hey, Dad, you OK?" I asked as I opened the door.

"More to the point, are you? I thought you'd be gone by now."

"Yeah, I was looking for the keys. I'm fine, Dad. You go in. I'll see you tomorrow."

I waited for him to enter the house before closing the car door. I slammed the cellphone to my ear again.

"Gabriel. You still there?"

"Yes, I'm still here…"

"You're gonna have to come down here to get…"

He stopped me in mid-sentence. "Helena, just turn the ignition switch."

"But…?"

"It'll work. Just try it," he said, as if he could hear my thoughts.

"How? I've got no keys," I queried, logically.

Without the keys, how could it possibly start?

"Hels, please just try it. It'll work."

"OK."

I smiled to myself, thinking this is just not going to work; there is no reason for it to, but here goes anyway. I quickly turned the switch to start the engine. My fingers tingled. It was like pins and needles in the tips. I pulled my hand away to try and rub the tingling sensation away. My concentration was on myself for a moment and so I missed the fact that the engine was actually running idly. It was my foot on the accelerator, gently increasing the noise in the engine, that brought my attention back on track. "I don't believe it. How did…?"

My attention was diverted to the noise coming from my cell-phone on the passenger seat. I grabbed it.

"Gabriel. You there?"

"Yes, I'm here, Helena. How'd you get on?"

"It worked. I don't believe it but it worked. The car started. How did...?" I was still in shock. I couldn't believe what just happened.

"See you soon," he said, so matter-of-fact, as if what just happened, a miracle of sorts, was of no importance to him.

I dropped my phone in the overnight bag placed on the seat beside me. The drive seemed to take minutes. It may have been longer but it seemed to go by in a flash. I didn't remember getting that far. The journey was a bit of a blur. I was still in a state of shock at being able to drive in the first place. I pulled up outside the house. I could see the light shining throughout.

The last of the dusk had disappeared and complete darkness replaced it. I reached for my bag, at the same time reaching with the other hand to turn off the ignition switch, but quickly pulled back at the memory of my previous experience. My fingers had only just got their feelings back. I spied Gabriel standing in the porch as I opened the car door. The engine died, the lights on the dashboard were out, but I never got to turn them off, so how? I turned back to Gabriel, hoping for answers I guess, of which I got none.

"You coming in, then?" Gabriel said, meeting me at the car door.

I couldn't speak as I climbed out of the seat to greet him.

"Helena, you coming in?" I think he sensed I was preoccupied.

"Yeah."

My mind was still dealing with the previous episode, so I was not fully aware of my actions right now.

"Did you see that?" I managed to say. I was still stunned by it all. I didn't expect him to answer. After all I wasn't making much sense.

"Yes. Don't worry about that now. I'll explain all of that later," he said, as he closed the car door behind me. "Come on in," he repeated, and I followed him into the house.

"But did you see how it switched itself...?" I stopped mid-sentence.

"I know. I'll explain in a minute. Let's just get inside, OK?" he finished, as I slumped down in one of the easy chairs in the lounge.

It was strange being back in his house again after all this time. The last time was when I came looking for him, the day he disappeared. The temperature hadn't changed. It was still freezing in there. And Gabriel must have sensed it, as he quickly made reference to it. The fire was lit in no time. How he did that so quickly was beyond me. It was as though the succession of tasks was all done in a blink of an eye, too fast to notice until it was completed. He was back before I knew it.

"I see you've brought a travelling bag. Any reason for that?" he asked curiously as he took a seat opposite me.

"Oh, yeah. Well I thought, if you don't mind, perhaps I could stay over?"

He said nothing, looking a little puzzled at my request. An explanation would have been good now but to be honest, I hadn't thought of a reason for staying.

"I thought maybe it'll give us a chance to talk undisturbed. And of course it'll save you a journey in taking me back, seeing that you're ill and all that."

He shot me a smile, indicating that he understood.

"I see. Well, that makes sense. You seemed to have worked it all out. Although you might find it too cold here, though. We haven't had guests in..." He stopped short. "How about ever. No, we've never had any guests, so you're the first," he finished.

"Well, then I am honoured," I said, smirking at him.

And he returned the gesture.

"Don't worry, I'll be fine," I said to reassure him.

He shook his head in agreement, as his face shined with such brightness. I had so missed that quality of his.

23

A Shared Secret

We sat for some time, chatting and laughing about things. I had missed that part of our relationship. It was so great being around him again. The fire had transformed the house into a cosy environment. I felt totally relaxed.

Gabriel showed me my room for the night. It had an air of just what he had said: no life in it for a long while, a feeling of history, of time and people gone by. I imagined the kind of guests his family had staying here; probably rich people. I remembered the pictures on the walls downstairs and had an insight into that feeling. Gabriel's mannerisms and the way he dressed also gave me good reason to think that way.

Between the two of us we sorted out the room, making it more habitable. The bedding was old. Frills hung from the edge of the sheets. There was no duvet, just blankets. I was thinking about what Gabriel had said, about the cold in here. Looking at the bedding, I thought he might have been right.

"I'll put some blankets over here in the chair, just in case," he said, as if he could read my mind.

"Yeah, thanks!"

Gabriel made his exit, as I heard the faint sound of ringing inside my bag.

"That's your father ringing, making sure you're OK," Gabriel said, walking out of the room.

How did he know that?

I rummaged through the bag, looking for the light that illuminated my phone in the dark surroundings, amongst the other life possessions I had thrown in. I really must sort this out someday, I thought.

"I'll see you downstairs," Gabriel said, closing the door behind him.

"OK," I said, still frantically looking for the phone. It'll stop in a minute; I'll be out of time, I thought. I always had that feeling. Maybe if I didn't have so much crap in here I'd find it easier. With that thought, I threw the contents onto the bed. Found it! I grabbed it and quickly flipped the lid to answer.

"Hi, Dad." Anxiety came to a head. I'd caught it in time.

"Baby. You OK? I just wanted to make sure you got there OK," he said as I began to chill out again.

"Yeah, Dad, I'm fine."

How did he know that? Was it a lucky guess? How could Gabriel possibly know? It was weird. I stopped, my mind running amuck.

"How's Gabriel feeling?" Dad asked.

"Yeah, he's a lot better now. He thinks it's something he ate." I smiled at that thought, considering that on the occasions I'd seen him eat, he never did much of it.

"He didn't mind you staying over, then?" Dad asked inquisitively.

"No, he was fine with it. In actual fact, what with him not feeling a hundred percent, he thought it a good idea."

This expanding of the truth was getting a little too easy, I thought.

"I told you I could have followed you there, brought you back," Dad said.

The tone of his voice had changed. He sounded flippant and

slightly annoyed. At what I wasn't sure, but maybe the idea of me staying here didn't particularly go down well.

"I know, Dad, but I wanted to check he was all right and I couldn't do that in a few minutes, could I? Especially with you hanging around outside for me. It would be rude," I explained, hoping I'd covered all the angles.

"Right, I see what you mean. Well, you say hello for me." He sounded a little defeated.

"Yeah, I will, Dad. See you tomorrow. Love you!"

"Love you too, baby."

I heard the silence of the ended call.

Gabriel was waiting when I arrived downstairs. He threw me a smile of acknowledgement.

"Everything all right?" he asked as I took my seat.

"Yeah, he's OK. He asked me to say hello."

"Is he OK about you being here?" he asked, as though he had sensed Dad's feelings about me being here.

"Yeah, he's fine about it. In fact, he was more worried about you."

He threw me an inquisitive look.

"Well, I had to give him an excuse for the party earlier. So I told them you were ill," I explained. "Hence that's why he asked."

His expression was one of praise, I guess, for my quick thinking.

"I see. Well, that's nice of him, even if I'm not ill as such," he replied.

"Yeah, but I really hate lying to him and I seem to be doing it a lot lately."

"Well, it's not really lying as such," Gabriel said.

I now must have looked inquisitive.

"Rather, it's exaggerating the truth," he said.

"How's that?" I said, more confused at his thinking.

"Well in a way, I have been ill. I've not exactly been myself, have I?" He gave me a little quizzical smile.

I gave it some thought. Yeah, he was right. It wasn't so far from the truth.

"Yes?" he asked.

"If you put it like that."

I glanced at my watch, not being able to see a clock anywhere around. It was late. Only another thirty minutes and we'd be into the early hours of the morning. We had talked all night but never touched on any past events. In fact it was such a relaxed time that it never came up, although it was always lingering in the back of my mind to raise in conversation.

"Helena, I know you have lots of questions for me but it's really late."

I was taking note of the time on my watch. So he knew then, that I had things to say.

"And there are things I must tell you but tonight, or shall I say this morning, may not be the right time," he went on.

"Yeah, you're right. Maybe tomorrow would be better," I agreed, although I was a little curious to know what he had to say to me.

He smiled.

"In that case, I think I'll go up. It's been a really busy day, what with the graduation and the party tonight."

"Yes, I forgot. How did the ceremony go? Sorry I wasn't able to be there for you," he said.

"It was OK. You know me. I hate too much fuss. I think my Mum would have loved it though."

I don't know what made me think about her then. I sighed and thought about that image for a while.

"You OK?" Gabriel asked, studying my face. "You know,

Helena, she would have been really proud."

I shot him a smile. "Thanks! Well, OK. I'm done. I'll see you in the morning. Thanks for letting me stay," I said as I stood up to go upstairs.

He stood himself, to greet me, his hands grabbing mine. I wasn't expecting that. The mood between us all night had been casual, friendly, but certainly with no signs of anything else.

"I've been wanting to do that all night," he confessed.

I bowed my head and smiled with embarrassment. Unknown to him I had the same feelings running through me. He placed one hand under my chin to lift it. The glow of his smile radiated out of him. He bent his head, placing his cheek against mine. My heart was pounding heavily but my body was flightless, as if I was floating off somewhere.

"Stay with me," he whispered, as if he could feel this too.

He lifted his face ever so slightly, so we faced each other, both hands cupping my face. He stared into my eyes as if to search for something. My heart felt like it was going to explode. My body was floppy, out of control.

"Helena, I…" He stopped and searched my face once more, one of his smiles escaping.

He bent his head towards me and my eyes closed, without thought or reason, my heart thumping all the while. I felt him there so close to my mouth now, his lips touching mine ever so gently. I wanted to push my lips harder against his but the moment was so tender, I didn't want to spoil it.

"Helena?"

The light was so white around us as I opened my eyes. I could see nothing else at first, just bright white light, with no sign of him, but I was comfortable being here. Moments later, the light started to fade.

"Helena?"

I could hear his voice, distant at first, but then nearer as his face came into focus, his famous smile etched all over it.

"You OK?" he asked.

I couldn't speak at first. My heart was still racing from the excitement within it. I shook my head in acknowledgement.

"See you in the morning," I said, more as a statement than a question.

"Hmm!" he acknowledged, releasing my hands as I made my way upstairs.

I could hear talking in the background; maybe two people, a man and a woman, their voices so soft. The light was so bright. I searched for the voices as they spoke to one another. I walked silently so as not to disturb them. However the action was not like walking; it was not as clumsy a task, more a graceful movement, like gliding. I sensed I'd had this feeling before. I wasn't afraid, more curious than anything else. They were getting closer. I reached out my arms, the white light taking them, wanting to touch something, anything that would resemble a person there. In a moment the scene changed. The white light was replaced by warm daylight, beams of sunshine streaming down from above. I could feel that warmth on my face as I approached some steps leading up to a stage.

Climbing felt so heavy on my legs as I willed myself to reach the top. A man of middle age dressed in formal robes stood at the top waiting. He handed me an object, a long, white paper document rolled up and tied with a bright red ribbon. I soaked up the sun's strength as I strode the length of the stage, hearing familiar voices in the crowd. I searched for clarity.

Piercing whistles and thunderous clapping kept me focused. I watched as the sun centred itself in a certain area, there to the right, amongst the crowd. I searched the warmth. It was so familiar to me now. I wanted it to dim, so I could see what was behind it. The presence was strong, something I knew well. I blinked, trying to re-focus. It seemed a heavy task, concentrated even, as if I was desperately wanting to see through that blink. My dad was there, smiling and clapping, harder and louder than any other, so it seemed, his pride showing for all to see. I could feel the overwhelming warmth of his love and I embraced it. The intensity of the sun that shone next to him was dimming slightly, rather like a glow when the sun goes down at the end of the evening. A feeling of curiosity remained within me, as my mind focused on the light. Shadow soon replaced it and I could see more clearly now.

The sun didn't hurt my eyes any more and I was able to see around me. Dad was still smiling. It gave me a glow of warmth inside, as I glanced at the object that was by my dad's side. A well-dressed man with familiar features now occupied one side of him. Gabriel was that man and on the other… My wish had come true! I could feel my smile widen with excitement at the scene that now faced me. My focus swapped to the other side. And it was here that I was greeted by the image of my mother seated next to my father. I had forgotten how beautiful she was, her smile so radiant, her hair as black as a raven. She was wearing her favourite summer dress. Dad had bought it for her on one of our holidays. She had loved it from the moment she saw it. She said the bright colours made her feel free. I could feel her gaze on me as she smiled the warmest of smiles, telling me all she wanted to without saying a word. They had seen me after all. A breath of coldness touched my face as I watched the vision in front of me fade.

Eyes wide, I sensed someone was there in front of me, my memory of where I was momentarily lost. I focused on the very dim light beside me, mistaking shadows for something more important in the room, half scaring myself to death. It wasn't until I moved slightly that I realised I was in a bed, but knew it was not my own. As I re-focused my vision, I could feel the weight of someone sat beside me, remembering very quickly I was in Gabriel's house.

"You awake?" he asked, repositioning himself.

I didn't see him at first. He wasn't inside the shadow of the light. I lifted my head up slightly to see where he was, sensing he'd moved closer.

"What are you doing here?" I asked curiously, my head still all over the place. I could still piece together bits of what was clearly a dream.

The light was brighter now, as if someone had put on the main light. I felt him even closer. I felt awkward in front of him, maybe because of where I was and having a lot less clothing on than I was used to. Being this close to him was my weakness. I moved further up the bed, as he readjusted himself next to me.

"I heard you call out. I thought something was wrong."

"Did I?" I searched myself for answers.

"I've been here awhile, just watching you," he said.

"Really?" I was still searching my memory.

"Yeah. You were saying stuff in your sleep. It was quite interesting actually, watching you."

"I can't believe for one moment that anything I do is that interesting to watch." I tried to visualise Gabriel studying my facial expressions, my breathing, everything. Most people would find that stuff real boring but not Gabriel; he thrived on things like that. "What was I saying then? Did it make any sense?" I asked, trying to get an idea of what he might have experienced from watching me.

"Yes, you mentioned your mother."

And then it came to mind. I sat up straight.

"Helena?"

"Yeah, I remember now." I could still see images of them sat there, together.

"It was my graduation and both of you were sat there in the audience with my father."

He said nothing.

"I obviously have a very overactive mind but it was great while it lasted." I wrapped my arms around my knees and tucked them up under my chin. The memory seemed so surreal but perfect nonetheless.

"Do you want a drink, now that you are awake?"

"Yeah, love one," I said, as I swung my legs out of the bed.

"I can bring it to you," he said.

"No, it's OK. I'll come with you," I said as I grabbed my coat to put round me.

I felt the cold of the house on my legs as I followed Gabriel downstairs.

"Cold?" he asked.

"Yeah, a little."

It was strange. I didn't see it happen, but one minute he was ambling down the stairs and the next he was gone. By the time I'd reached the bottom and was walking into the lounge, the fire had been lit and he was stood in the kitchen. How was he able to do that? And so quick! I never felt a thing. Puzzling.

"You OK?" he asked.

"Yeah, fine." I was still thinking about what had just happened. I wondered whether he realised how fast he seemed at times. This needed some answering! I sat myself down on the couch, legs curled up under my chin, arms wrapped around them. God! This house is cold! Seconds later Gabriel was back with drinks.

"It'll soon warm up in here," he stated.

"Sit here, next to me. You can keep me warm for a bit," I pleaded, continuing the rocking motion. Even the fabric on the couch was cold. I should have stayed in bed, although that also took me a little while to get comfortable.

He sat next to me, slowly extending his arm to my shoulder but resting it very lightly as if not to be noticed.

"Better?" he asked.

"Yeah." My teeth were chattering and I tried to bury my body in his side.

"It'll be better in a minute," he said, trying to reassure me.

I turned my head to look at him. He did not meet my gaze. I could feel the tension in his body, all stiff and formal-like.

"Tell me something. How do you do that?" I said, wanting to know his secret, how he was so quick at things, lighting the fire and being in the kitchen, all within a split second of me getting to the bottom of the staircase. Was it my imagination?

I sensed a little awkwardness in him; not that he moved or anything but there was a noticeable distance for sure.

"Come on then, how did you?" I demanded, searching his face for some sort of an answer from him.

I felt his arm pull away from my shoulder. He laid it in his lap. He looked so sullen and sad, pained in some way.

"You OK?" I asked, a little concerned at his sudden change of mood.

He didn't say anything; he just carried on staring into his lap as if he was a million miles away.

"Gabriel?" I moved my head closer to him, confused at this behaviour.

He stood and moved to the chair opposite, sitting on the edge, looking ill at ease, his body posture showing something was wrong. I remained where I was, and he finally looked up at me with what could only be described as conviction in his eyes.

"Helena?"

"Yes."

"I told you there was something I needed to talk with you about," he started.

"So you want to talk now?" I asked.

"Yes, if that's OK with you?"

His sad look had gone, only to be replaced by a troubled expression. I could see that things were ticking over in his mind.

"Look, Gabriel, just say it. What's wrong?"

"I just don't know how to put this," he said.

"It doesn't matter. Just tell me." Although I said it, a part of me was a little nervous. Was he about to chuck me?

"Your friend, Rob, he was right," he said, looking from me to his lap again, his hands clasped together, hanging over the ends of his knees.

I hated seeing him in this state, so vulnerable and alone. However, I was confused at his statement. What was he right about?

"What do you mean?" I asked.

I studied him for a moment, watching his facial expressions change, as if he was battling with himself. He seemed to be at odds with himself, confused even.

"That time in the diner, when he couldn't see me, you remember? And the time at the hospital; he wasn't able to see me either. Your workmate, the day we went to the cinema. I watched you both as you looked towards me that day. I was puzzled but now I realise that she couldn't see me either, could she?" he said, his eyes expressing strong curiosity.

My mind was awash with all this stuff he had bombarded me with. I searched my memories for those times he had so precisely listed out. It seemed such a long time ago now.

"Yes I do, but how did you know that the cinema thing? I never said anything to you about it," I said. I knew there was no way he could have heard us from where he was standing.

"I sensed something wasn't right when you both looked at me. You were talking about me to her, weren't you?"

"Yes." His statement almost made me feel I was saying things I shouldn't have. I needed to explain myself. "I said I was watching a film with you and yes, you're right, she told me she couldn't see you. As you can imagine I was a little confused as I could see you perfectly well. I wasn't about to make a fuss, not with everyone there, so I had to make an excuse, suggesting perhaps you'd gone to the little boys room," I explained.

"So, you've known that something hasn't been right for a long while?" he said, his tone sounding rather accusing. I'd not seen this side of him before.

"Well, yes I guess so. But it doesn't make sense. How is it that I'm able to see you? And then there's Dad, for that matter." I was confused with the whole thing, very much as I had been before today, all those months ago when I first told him. I remembered how difficult it was to even say the words, knowing that I could not make sense of it, and still today I was no clearer. Fear and confusion were instantly etched on his face as he took in the meaning of my words. But neither of those elements was present today. The previous months of anger within him had been replaced with understanding and perhaps empathy for himself.

"I don't know why. Sometimes it happens that way for some of us," he said, looking at me with real meaning in his face.

I had not expected this change in him. In fact, although I had wanted answers to these questions, I was somewhat unsure as to how he would react again when bringing them up.

"What do you mean by that? Who's we?" I was trying to piece

things together, to get a handle on this. Yes, I knew that it was strange in itself that people couldn't see him but I was sensing there was something else to this which I hadn't sussed out yet.

"I'm not as you see me," he said. "I'm different!" he blurted out, as I watched him search my face for a reaction.

I was so confused. What on earth was he going on about? Different? But I already knew that. And wasn't that what I liked?

"Look, Gabriel, I really don't know what you're trying to say. Just tell me!"

Frustration on his face, he rubbed his hands together, as if he was irritated by the situation. This seriously wasn't easy for him that was for sure!

"It really can't be that bad, so just get on with it," I said, a little frustrated myself. I was instantly aware that I sounded rather flippant. It wasn't my intention, but in trying to keep up with this whole guessing game, my patience was waning. "So?"

"OK!" he said, with some conviction in his voice. "You see me, right?" His irritation remained.

"Yes, of course!"

"I know now what they say is true. The others I mean. At first when you told me, I was angry and confused at what you were telling me. It didn't make any sense to me. Yes, I knew there were things in my life, strange things that had happened since coming back here, that I couldn't understand, but I never questioned it. I guess because I was afraid of what it meant. Scared of being someone different, of not being normal. For the first time in my life, I felt I belonged. But now, things make more sense to me. I know who I am."

I didn't say anything in response. I couldn't. I was still stumbling over the pieces, pulling together all that he had just said, trying to make sense of it.

"Helena? I sense in your eyes what I know I must tell you, but this is not easy for me to say to you. I fear only one thing now. That it will change everything," he said, looking away.

"What will? Please just tell me. Who are you?" I snapped, impatiently.

"I am an angel, Helena!" His voice was soft and sincere.

"An angel!"

The room fell silent.

24

Reality Check

No further words were exchanged between us for a moment. His anxiety as he waited, no doubt, for some sort of response from me, was plain for me to see. But my head was all over the place. None of it made any sense. Past events were toing and froing through my mind as I looked for some evidence of truth in what Gabriel had said. A part of me said what he was talking about was ridiculous, but certain events that had happened when Gabriel had been around me, I knew needed some explanation. The time when we were having a meal at the diner, after the cinema episode, I thought odd when the waitress didn't address him at all. She seemed to be talking to me only, even though Gabriel was sat there opposite me, and yet she seemed to treat the situation as if I was a single customer. Thinking about it now, I could see the tell-tale signs of things that weren't quite right. Had Gabriel had these thoughts also but dismissed them as I had? But to say what he did really was unbelievable.

"I take it that you mean this in the strictest sense?" I was being flippant in a way, trying to hide my uncertainty that this could be in any way true.

He caught my gaze. His face said it all. A disappointed reaction that said, "If only this was easier."

I realised I'd made a mistake right there in making that comment.

"Yes!"

"I'm sorry, Gabriel, but I really don't get it. If you are what you say you are…"

He cut me off swiftly. "An angel!" he said quite sharply. He really was trying to make the point.

"Yeah, whatever!" I couldn't quite comprehend that this person was what he said he was. Maybe it was fear that made me so confrontational. He just couldn't be. "So if you are that…" Even trying to say the word sounded wrong. "How is it that I can see you, and Dad for that matter, but no one else can? I mean, what you are telling me is that you are some kind of ghost, entity, thing. Is that right? So how does that work? I thought angels were some kind of myth, not real, but here you are flesh and blood for me to touch and feel. Gabriel, I don't understand; it doesn't make sense to me."

I could see the bombardment of questions I was throwing in his direction was an irritation to him. I thought about my actions. Was I being thoughtless, challenging, uncaring, at a time perhaps Gabriel needed my understanding and tact?

"You have to understand, Helena. I had a whole different life mapped out for me in my head. So to know that it is not going to play out in the same way has been difficult for me. Building up to telling you has been my most difficult task, though. I know you are finding it difficult to take in, to get your head around it, but believe me, it is no more than I went through when I was first told," he said.

"How long have you known?" I asked softly. He had been carrying this around and he never told me. Why?

It was noticeable that his posture was slightly more relaxed now. He'd stopped wringing his hands together and had moved back more in his seat.

"I always knew somehow that coming back here to Teignmouth was different for me. Meeting you was like a calling or something but I had no understanding of why. Any unusual thoughts I had about myself, I disregarded. But in the back of my mind, I knew something wasn't right. I could feel it. So when you told me about your friend not being able to see me, well, yes, I was angry at first, but I think mainly at myself because it was yet another tell-tale sign that something was amiss with me. I felt a sham, thinking I was something that I was not – normal. All my life I had only spent time with my family; no friends, no other persons until you. You gave me what I had missed so long: companionship, love and passion, things I had never felt before and I wasn't about to let that go. Everything I had come to know was slipping away. I could feel it but I didn't know why. And then it was revealed to me, the day you were supposed to see me here. We were going to talk about the situation. Do you remember?" he asked.

"Yeah, that's right. I called up but you were nowhere to be seen. When I got here the door was wide open. I checked everywhere for you, I mean everywhere. I even checked upstairs in your wardrobe. I thought perhaps you'd gone somewhere but everything was in its place. It was so weird! It was as though you'd just disappeared. So I just put it down to that you had been called away to your aunt's in a hurry. That would then explain the door being open and no phone calls from you, like the last time. Remember!"

I shot him a smile, hoping it would lighten his load. But it didn't.

"The clothes thing was strange though. That bugged me for a while before I convinced myself that you had others at your aunt's. And that got me through. You said it was revealed to you. When?" I asked.

"Like I said, it happened just before you came, I guess," he replied.

"But I don't understand. What happened?" I asked curiously.

"The day you came up, when the door was open. It was just before that. I had a visit from her. I thought it was you at first but then I was shown it was something quite different."

"Her? Who you talking about?" I asked, trying to keep up.

"My mother!" He paused for a moment. "She was my visitor."

I was confused. I thought she was dead. "But how is that possible? I thought you said your mother was, well, you know."

"Dead? Yes, she is but she was sent to show me the way. It was time," he said.

"What do you mean, it was time?"

"Time for me to learn who and what I was. Am!" he said softly, looking at me for some reassurance that I was at last getting some kind of handle on all of this.

"So, where did you go? What was it like?"

I watched as he searched his mind, looking to piece memories together.

"I remember having a strange sensation run through me. It was bright, blindingly so, but comforting at the same time. My body felt weightless and my mind drifted out of time and reason. It's difficult to truly explain what really happened at that moment but I just remember how relaxed I felt, at one with myself. I never questioned myself, like I did here, I just accepted it. It was as though I already knew this part of me. In fact I felt I always had. I was not confused with who I was; it was not a shock, it was a comfort. I finally knew who I was! As time went on, my mother was able to give me an understanding of the things that I had questions for and all the things I didn't. I was like you at first, dismissive, but I knew that some things needed explanation for the way in which things happened whilst I've been back here."

"So, your mother, she's what? The same as you then? An angel?"

"Yes, my family has a long history apparently; it goes back

centuries. It was hard at first to even accept all of this stuff being said about me, let alone all the other stuff about our heritage. It was said that my mother was the first of our kind. For centuries it was believed that this gift was never given to females, that only males had the right to be chosen. There were many sacrifices made. To be gifted in this way meant you were chosen to do the bidding for one man alone, and to that aim it was forbidden to marry. But my mother was different; she was not born of the gift, she was given it."

"But why?" I was sensing there was a lot more to this.

"It was a very long time ago. I don't know the exact details but it was sometime before my father was on the scene. Like I said I'm not sure, it's only what I've heard from others of us. It's like some sort of big, dark secret that no one dares mention. But my mother was given this gift for the wisdom she showed a person at a time when it was crucial for them."

"So who was this person? She must have done something really important for this person to be given such a gift, especially when it is forbidden. And what about your father then? You say this was before him. I'm a little confused, Gabriel, I thought you said that males were unable to marry. And I don't understand, your mother and father, how?"

I watched as Gabriel's expression changed from comfortable to defeated. He looked very much like that little detail had missed him completely.

"OK, so how do you feel knowing you are an angel?" I said, trying to cover up the silence from him, and finding it surprisingly less difficult to say than before.

"Let's just say it was easier being with my own kind but here, being a part of this life, you, it's just so difficult. To be honest, I'm scared as hell! Pardon the phrase."

We laughed so hard, it hurt. It was great just to lose the intensity for a minute. In a weird kind of way, I was OK about it. Of course I sensed things were different about him from the beginning, so in a strange way it wasn't such a big surprise. Yeah, I was a little distant from him when I realised the strangeness was noticed by others, but time elapsed to digest all of that and put it into perspective. The idea of him being an angel was really OK. Yes, I knew I didn't understand the meaning of that. Thoughts of Gabriel being a dead man, walking around, communicating with me, were all milling around in my head somewhere. Apart from that he looked and sounded no different; he was still the same guy, the same Gabriel I loved.

"I guess I feel better than I did. Especially having told you. It was really hard not being able to find the right words but now I feel relieved. I'm dealing with the fact of who I am and what that means a little at a time, but my emotions, which I learnt from you apparently, have at times made it difficult to focus the way I should," he said, looking at me.

I leant my head to one side, instantly realising what he was saying, knowing what I knew now made sense.

"You know, how we always have a sense of what each other is feeling? And before it was OK, it was allowed but now, we just can't have those feelings. It's not appropriate for me any more," he said.

I felt like the world caved in on me right at that moment.

"What do you mean, not appropriate? How can you just switch off your feelings like that? 'Cause I sure as hell can't." I could feel my heart raging with disappointment, torture, for what this would do to me, being around him but meaning nothing more than any other person.

"Helena, you must understand, I asked for this, to be given the assignment of being your guardian angel! It was my only way of staying by your side, to watch you every day. And with it comes a responsibility, to guide and protect you from those things that intend to lead you on a different path. A journey in which I may not follow. In time to come the journey you take will be chosen for you; it will be right and true and the right road for you and it will be a time for me to take my leave of you until if and when you have need of me again, but what we have had, the relationship, the bond, cannot remain. It must now change," he said, pleading for me to understand but with great sadness at the content of his declaration.

His words pained me as I digested them.

"What do you mean, change? Why? You can't." I felt so desperate listening to him talk about us in that way. The way he said it had a definitive meaning behind it: our friendship was finished. How could that be, just because of who he was? It didn't make any sense.

"Helena, I am an angel!" He said it like he was stating a strong point.

"Yes, yes. I know all of that," I said flippantly, as I stood up sharply. "But why should that change anything between us?"

He also stood and took my hands in his own.

"Helena?" He looked deep into my eyes. So angelic and with real meaning. I sensed so much sadness lingering in his face. And at that point I understood that his pain was just as deep as mine. "These feelings I have for you, Helena, sadly can no longer be."

I heard each of his words spoken so softly but they hit me like a thousand knives, the pain searing through me with such intensity.

"But, Gabriel, I love you!" I felt the warmth from my tears as they cascaded down my face.

"Hels, I know."

He raised his hand to cup the side of my face, his angelic eyes piercing mine with such affection and a deep sense of disappointment at the same time.

"Do you not feel the same?" I asked, desperately wanting him to take me in his arms and hold me closer, telling me it was all a mistake.

"Yes! With all my heart, but then you know that, Hels. You know all my feelings," he replied with a vulnerable look on his face.

He was right, I did know all his thoughts, right down to the ones he was having right now, and I could clearly see he was struggling with this himself.

"If we feel this way, why must it change?" I asked, knowing that deep down it wasn't as simple as that. I needed to make him see that this was a desperate situation and I was scared of the decisions that he was taking on behalf of us both.

"Hels, please! This is hard enough," he said pleadingly.

"God, I'm so sorry!" I hated seeing him this way, pained and helpless, unable to keep what we wanted and to achieve what he had to do. No words were exchanged, just a look, a shared moment within that look that reflected the turmoil going on inside us both. He released his hand from my face and my head leant forward onto his chest. I could feel the warmth of his arms encased around my shoulders as his chin rested on the top of my head.

"How can this be, Gabriel?" I said under my breath. Thoughts were rushing through me, telling me that the feelings I had for this person could be nothing less than what they were, and that I was frightened of what the future held for me without him. This whole thing just wasn't fair!

"I know, Helena, I know," he replied in gasps while kissing the top of my head.

We stayed that way for quite a while, in what seemed like a rocking motion, without a word said between us. I sensed the heaviness of his embrace, which seemed to acknowledge the burden he had to bear. His face moved down beside mine. His hand reached to rest on the back of my head, as if to cradle it. I could feel my body take on a tingling sensation, as I felt his warmth embrace the nape of my neck.

"I'm sorry, Helena," I heard him whisper softly in my hair.

I looked up from his chest as my head rested in the crook of his hand. In those few seconds that passed, no words could surpass all the emotions that ignited within us now. The sorrow engulfed me as I stared into his eyes and felt its overwhelming energy. The pain that followed grabbed at my chest as my heart pounded with every breath. I knew he felt it too. It was there in his eyes, etched in the frown on his face. The energy that was held within that embrace was just too much to bear. His face moved slowly, inch by inch, towards mine, as my reaction mirrored his. The softness of his lips touched mine and my body lit up like a fireworks display. The moment was so tender, but powerful at the same time. My heart was racing with excitement. This kiss told the story of our love for each other right there in that moment, but the pain within my heart, the longing for more, told me the ending wasn't so simple. I sensed that longing within Gabriel, as the acknowledgement of what he wanted and couldn't have was etched in the ending of that moment. His face was full of pain and anguish at the realisation.

"I'm so sorry, Hels! It's so difficult," he whispered, as he once again buried his head in my hair.

"It's not fair!" I blurted out softly, as we held each other.

But the moment didn't last long before I felt a change in Gabriel's stance, as he pulled away from me, holding both my hands in his. I could feel the distance between us grow. This was it, the start of things to come. He didn't say it but I knew deep down that there was change ahead.

"I think it's time we went back up, Helena."

My head was still in that embrace, feeling the warmth as he held my neck so perfectly in his hands. And yet now I was being brought back to reality, when I really just wanted to stay where I was.

"Hmm," I acknowledged, although deep down I didn't want to go anywhere and leave this moment. I sensed we wouldn't be able to get this feeling back again. There would be too many reasons to do as he asked.

He took the lead, hanging on to my hand, as we gently climbed the staircase, the heaviness of our thoughts weighing on our minds. I watched as the lights dimmed like magic behind us and I accepted it as if it was the norm. After being around Gabriel and hearing the news he had inflicted on me tonight, any little thing I would have once questioned held no query for me; it was all so normal now. But even though I accepted him as he was and the gift he had to give, would he allow himself to accept what he saw as abnormal? After all, technically, he was dead!

25

Acceptance

The rest of the early morning was spent lying in bed, thinking about the news that Gabriel had dropped on me during the night. It was difficult to understand the previous night, and the next day it seemed even more confusing. In my mind I replayed moments from the past, of when I had first met Gabriel. I tried to recall the situations when I realised there was something different about him. But that was just it; there were several times like that and I thought no more of them at the time. They were a part of who he was. I accepted it!

My thoughts were interrupted by a soft knock at the door, and I pulled myself up to a sitting position.

"Yeah?" I said, as I glanced at the window. The curtains were slightly parted, so I could see it was really bright out there. I quickly checked my watch for confirmation of the time and was surprised. It was only 7 a.m.

"Hi," Gabriel said, his walk silent as he made his way towards the bed and took a seat by my side. He was already dressed in one of his suits. Although he looked smart, my first impression was that it was a little over the top. But as always he smelt fantastic, his scent engulfing my face. I sensed his tension as he sat there, looking awkward, as if unsure what to say.

"Couldn't sleep?" he asked.

"No! Too much going on in my head," I said. "You?"

"The same," he replied.

174

"So, where do we go from here?" I asked him, as he put his head in his hands.

"I really don't know, Hels. I wish I had the answers."

"Look, Gabriel," I said, pulling myself up onto my knees behind him. He turned around to meet me, sadness so deep lingering in his eyes. "Why can't we just see how things pan out? Carry on as before. We both know there's going to be situations that we have to be careful about but I'm sure we can sort it out between us, don't you think?"

I could sense Gabriel thinking about what I had said. I felt his emotions heighten as he saw the possibilities of the idea I had put to him. But traditions always came into play, overshadowing his emotional needs. The building turmoil inside of him always brought him back to the same conclusion: this was something neither one of us could win.

"But things aren't the same, Hels. I'm not the same."

"You're not?" I said, moving closer towards him.

"Helena, you know I'm not. Who I am makes all the things we've had change."

"Not to me. Everything is the same for me. It makes no difference to me, what you are, who you are. In fact I feel so lucky having you around to look out for me," I said.

He moved around towards me, taking my hand in his as it lay in my lap. He stared down at my hand as he twiddled with my fingers, looking lost in his own little world.

"Gabriel?"

He looked up at me in response.

"You know, Helena, it's so surreal. I expected... well, actually I'm not sure what I expected, but not this anyway."

"I don't know what you're getting at." I was a little confused at his remark.

"You! Being so normal, as if nothing I told you this morning made a blind bit of difference."

"Well, that's good, isn't it?" I asked.

"No, not really. It just makes things harder for me to deal with." He returned his stare towards my hand again.

"So, what are you saying? You don't want me to be all right about all of this?" I asked, pulling my hand away from his.

"Yes, of course! It's not that. I don't really know what I'm saying. I just wish this was all easier, that's all."

I put my hand to his face, feeling the coolness of his skin as I guided it up towards mine. Watching the turmoil unfold within his eyes, I wished this wasn't as hard as it was for him.

"But, Gabriel, it can be, if only you let it," I whispered.

He grabbed my hand from the side of his face and held it in his own. Without thought he leant in towards me quickly and snatched a longing kiss from my lips. I felt his hunger, the strength of his passion burning inside his chest, as he pressed up against me. A mound of other emotions whizzed uncontrollably around inside of me. The moment stopped abruptly as Gabriel pulled away and stood up.

"Hels, I just can't. I can't do this. It's not fair to you or me. I need to keep focused and I can't do that in this way."

"But…"

He stopped me. "Helena, I can't. There's nothing more to be said. I'll meet you downstairs when you're done here. And I'll drop you back home."

I was surprised at how quickly his attitude had turned cold. It wasn't nasty or anything, just more of a hurt and dismissive reaction. I also sensed a hint of fear in his voice as he quickly made his exit. Before I could react, he was gone from the room.

It wasn't long before we'd pulled up alongside my house. And instantly I noted Dad had already gone to work. On the way here the conversation between us had been down to the bare minimum, reverting to yes-no answers when needed. But I didn't want to push it. I could see the turmoil in his eyes and feel the desperation in his voice. The engine was left ticking over for a few moments and then fell silent. He sat still, just staring at the windscreen. The silence was deafening, intimidating even, as I trawled my mind for something to say, anything that would break this void. But for all my willingness to open my mouth and say it, hesitation took over and left me there still wanting him to want me, like he once did, to make this right as before. The air inside was awkward. It was difficult to judge what each of us was thinking. The confined space was clouded by complications, thick with them. I sensed no way through, no glimmer of hope, so I grabbed my bag and opened the passenger door to make my exit.

"See ya!" I said in passing, without thinking about it. They didn't seem the right words to say; so uncaring, insensitive perhaps, leaving no room for discussion. But that atmosphere left me feeling a little empty of anything else to say, still pulling at my bag.

It was stuck. I kept pulling at it, tutting to myself with embarrassment, unable to concentrate on doing what was necessary to release it. If only I could have stopped and thought about it, but the frustration mixed with the overwhelming sense of embarrassment at not making this an easy task was unbearable. I could feel the glow in my face rise to my head, making it hot and sticky, anger swelling up inside me in turn, leaving me so tight and knotted I just wanted to scream at that moment and break that silence, and all over a bag! I stopped, deflated, and at that moment I felt the touch of his warm hand, and instantly my grip on the handles loosened.

"Helena! Please! Stop!" His voice was soft and sullen but very reassuring.

I turned back around in my seat and looked at his grip, taking a long look at him as he stared softly at me. I relaxed in my seat.

"Please! I'm sorry," he said, as I pulled my legs back into the car, sensing there was more for him to say. "It's so hard, all of this!" he added, sounding deflated.

"I know it is but, Gabriel, ruining what we have is surely not the answer either. Does it not mean anything to you?" I asked. However, I realised as soon as I said it that it was insensitive of me. I knew the demons he was fighting; he was striving to put things right between us yet also to follow what was required of him. Not a decision I had to make.

"Of course it does. You know it does, but I'm bound by the rules I must follow. Our kind is not permitted to have any kind of relationship. I'm strictly here to serve a purpose." His head hung down, his voice left empty, as if he had nothing left to give.

"You're not permitted to fall in love?" I asked, and then I remembered that he had touched on that subject when he was explaining his family history in the house. It had made no reference to me and Gabriel at the time, but now it was making more sense.

"No! It's against our heritage. No love, no relationships, no marriages, nothing that resembles a normal human life." Pointing it out to me just made him more sullen.

I hated seeing him this way, stricken and confused, not at one with himself as I had always known him to be.

"I think the best thing would be to not see each other any more."

His words dropped like an explosion.

He turned towards me, searching for my reaction to his words, his eyes watching mine, sad but waiting, perhaps, for my protests of disapproval. But my body had gone into meltdown at the mere idea of him never being around me again. I just couldn't conceive my life continuing without him in it. I was in total shock. I didn't see that coming.

Yes, I knew things would be difficult but this, not being able to see him ever, how would I cope? He was a big part of my life now.

"Is that what you want then?" I said calmly, knowing deep down that it wasn't, but what alternative did he have?

"No, Helena! But what other choice do I have?" He looked meaningfully at me, as if willing me to come up with an alternative. As much as I needed to find it, I knew I had nothing to offer.

"Hmm, well, you must do what you feel you have to," I said, no doubt sounding as defeated as I felt.

The car fell silent, as the words whizzed around in our heads, neither of us really wanting to commit to what was the inevitable. The decision ultimately would be Gabriel's and I would have to agree, so as not to make this any more difficult a task than it already was. But my heart was broken, painfully so. I could feel its heaviness, lying in my chest, as I thought of trying to exist without his presence in my life. The idea of never seeing him again was just not even plausible.

"OK. Well, I'd better go," I said, as I felt the warmth of tears flowing easily down my face, desperately trying to shield them, not wanting to make this any worse. I grabbed my bag again and bent over towards him, my face tight with tears, still sticky with moisture, and gently kissed his cheek. I paused a moment. Such longing was stretched across his eyes, but he offered no words to suggest a change of mind. But the ability to do that was not in either of our hands. The thought of this ending here didn't seem real apart from the heavy pain lodged in my chest.

I climbed out of the passenger seat, my legs feeling like lead weights as I pulled them out onto the driveway. The car door closed slowly behind me. I hadn't noticed how heavy it had been before. It seemed like a tonne weight now, matching my heart. I tried not to focus on him as I stood there. I couldn't bear it, seeing his face etched with the same pain that had engulfed me. I could feel the intensity of his thoughts, a mishmash of pain, love, loss, rules and obligations. Although I couldn't see them, I could feel the heat of his tears as they welled in the bottom lid of his eyes, desperately waiting for him to blink, releasing the pressure that now lay there.

"Helena, please be safe!" I heard as he stretched towards the open passenger window.

Helena, just keep it together; just a few minutes more, I thought.

"Yeah, you too," I whispered, not sure if it was loud enough for him to hear, but my breath seemed to be struggling to release anything stronger. I turned towards the car. The engine's roar startled me as it started up, and before I had time to think the car pulled away. I watched as it neared the end of the road and turned the corner far too quickly before he disappeared out of sight. I felt the cold stone below me as I sat on the front step, head resting on top of my crossed arms, tears cascading uncontrollably down my face. The feeling of loss was so unbearable; the emptiness in my heart was overwhelmingly painful. The idea of never seeing him again was just inconceivable.

Several days passed. There was no contact from Gabriel, not that I expected any, but I had a little hope that there might be a chance of him changing his mind. But I reminded myself that that would be silly; he was doing what he had to do, what he was supposed to do. I spent most of my time in bed, lying around, my head still spinning from the whole thing. I had no goal, no purpose to this life without him in it. I kept replaying the moment he told me his news over and over, maybe hoping I could change the ending somehow. The sense of loss was the most difficult to deal with but this wasn't the first time. Gabriel had disappeared several times before, for no apparent reason, but I knew this was different. I knew it wasn't what we both wanted. That was the hardest part to accept. Watching the pain in his eyes that last day was so difficult. I knew he was fighting against his will to be with me.

My Dad didn't make it any easier at home either, being unaware that things had changed, but I made up some story to answer his questions about Gabriel. Of course, he noticed that Gabriel hadn't been around of late, and no doubt noticed my sombre mood. Whether or not he saw through my masquerade I don't know, but he never pursued the point once I gave my answers. Trying to go back to how it was before was difficult. Having all the answers to my questions about Gabriel had less appeal now, knowing that my friends and family would never really know the whole truth about him and what I knew was the reason for never being with him again. Also, it couldn't have come at a worse time, not that any time was good. But just finishing college and not being able to increase my hours at the picture house gave me plenty of time on my hands to think, and think some more. Before Gabriel had come back on the scene, Jamie had managed to get some tickets for the Glastonbury weekend. I'd forgotten all about it, what with everything going on once he was back, so when he reminded me on Facebook one night, it threw me. Part of me couldn't be bothered, but of course once Dad got whiff of it there was no way of getting out of it. And really we were lucky getting the tickets in the first place; they're like gold, everyone wants them. It's a massive music festival, with several strong bands playing; been going for years. So resisting was futile; nagging would definitely win the day and wear me down. And it did!

Finally the day arrived. We decided to leave for the massive muddy field in the heart of Somerset early Friday morning, hoping we'd miss heavy traffic congestion, but that was definitely wishful thinking, as we found out. Others had the same idea. I'd come prepared with my fashion designer wellies that I'd bought in a little, inexpensive shoe shop in Teignmouth. They even had the cheap designer label on them for all to admire as I brushed alongside celebs when I got there. Wellies were a must for the wet weather that made Glastonbury such an attraction. Usually the weather was mainly wet, wet and more wet, which adds up to a whole lot of muddy fields with thousands of tents bunched together.

Who would want to go through that? Yet, watching it on the TV over the years, you never got the impression that anyone was miserable; in fact, very much the opposite. It was just a big coming together of all ages just having a great time. Now that the hype was in full swing I was kind of looking forward to it. The unhappy thoughts of weeks gone by had all but disappeared, well for now anyway, but Gabriel was always there, in the back of my mind. I couldn't help wondering where he was now and what he was doing, whether he was happy or not. All these questions I would store away, but they would never be answered. As hard as it was I knew he was gone, was out of my life, and I needed to accept that and move on.

Having an early start was a good idea in theory, but the ground was already awash with people when we arrived, no doubt all having the same thought, as we joined the thousands of other hopeful people in the queue. The guys were pumping, charged and ready to go. They'd been going on about this for months, I think they were shocked they got the tickets in the first place; it was not an easy task. We pitched our tents in record time so we could be ready to wander around the attractions. We were off to a great start. The weather was holding up; the sun was shining and really quite warm. Fingers crossed, I might keep a dry sleeping bag tonight. I ambled around the many different stalls in the grounds, as I watched girls having their hair braided and henna tattoos being applied to people's anatomies, ready for an awesome weekend.

Our first day went so quickly, and surprisingly the sun remained all day and well into the evening. This was too good to be true; not the usual weather expected for the festival. Saturday seemed a whole lot busier; people still arriving, more tents emerging all the time. It was like camp city. Great fun though, so much better than seeing it on TV, although I'm not sure I would be saying the same if it was tipping down with rain and mud up to my waist, as it had been so often over the years. Wellies were the fashion accessories here; even the celebs got into the spirit. And this year, with no mud so far, the fashion logos were clearly visible. However, with the sun out so clearly on this festival, wellies weren't exactly the best option. Just as well I came prepared with some wishful thinking, with my converse shoes flat-packed well in my rucksack. I hadn't seen much of the boys. The night before they were getting acquainted with our neighbours in the surrounding tents. I didn't see much of them until the morning, crashed out on the grass, not managing to make it inside the tent, rather the worse for wear. The evidence of drinking outside their tent explained why. That left me to wander around on my own that morning, whilst they got over their hangovers. I had never been a big drinker, so it hadn't interested me to join in with them. This weekend for me was more about seeing my favourite band again. Muse's homecoming was awesome in Teignmouth last year and they were here playing again tonight. I couldn't wait. There was something for everybody here; an abundance of food and drink stalls, catering for all requests, a paradise of colourful trinkets, flags and pictures.

The sun had warmed up quite nicely as I headed back to the tent. Lying on the grass outside my tent, enjoying the warmth of the sun beating down on me, I felt comfort in the peace surrounding me. Most tents around us were still full with sleeping bodies. The sun was so soothing on my face as I soaked up its rays, enjoying my own little patch of paradise. But the feeling was soon interrupted by something familiar around me. My eyes searched automatically for something to explain these feelings but there was nothing solid, just feelings. A faint smell hung around me and this too was familiar. I tried to place it in my mind as I sat up. But everything was as it was around me; no change at all. So why the smell? It was a sweet, flowery aroma and it was getting stronger. Although it wasn't an alarming smell, it still frustrated me that I couldn't see the reason for it. Perhaps it was someone's perfume? In any case I had been interrupted, so I decided to take off for a wander, not before taking a quick look at the guys snoozing soundly in the tent. I made the assumption they probably would be there for most of the day, sleeping off the night's alcohol consumption. It was strange, though, how the smell still remained, as strong as before. I seemed to have brought it with me, as I wandered the grounds. The smell of cooked burgers and onions wafted through the air but never really disguised the sweet flowery smell.

There were masses of people everywhere as a result of the morning's arrivals. I could hear music playing from way in front of me. It was no doubt coming from one of the stages, and the emerging crowd heading that way confirmed that.

The afternoon came and went so quickly, considering I spent all of it on my own. The guys managed to get themselves up and eventually met me at one of the gigs. Although I surmised from looking at them that they were still suffering from hangovers, it was nothing that an extra pint of cider wouldn't cure. I was aware that the scent had remained with me all day. It was really strange, though, how the guys couldn't smell a thing. The highlight for me, however, had finally arrived. The band I had been waiting to see was up next. The area around the stage was packed and the sun was still shining. It couldn't have been better. Rob and Jamie had dragged me through the masses of fans in front of us. The place was buzzing; everyone was in the same mind. We pushed and shoved others around us as we managed to get as close to the front as was humanly possible. I wished I was taller at times like these. It was difficult enough stuck in a tight crowd, having to weave from side to side to get a glimpse of the band. Rob had offered to put me on his shoulders to get a better look, like some other people were doing, and I took him up on the idea immediately. There would be no chance of seeing a thing from down here once it got going. The scene was electric. Fans were singing their music, waiting for that first glimpse of the band as they entered the stage. And there they were! The noise was thunderous around us as the band leader, a musician of genius, strummed up a few chords on his glittering red guitar, and the rest of the band leapt into their set.

The weekend had just been fantastic but it had gone far too quickly. And the weather was the headline. It had turned out to be a scorcher, definitely not what was expected. I had time to reflect while it was quiet, as I watched the boys sleeping like babies on the back seat of the car. The drive home had been short. Surprisingly there was not much traffic on the road. I dropped the boys off first. By the looks of them they would be going straight to bed. Dad was home. I had rung him earlier to say we were on our way back. He said he was taking the day off, but didn't say why.

"Dad, I'm back," I said as I plonked my stuff on the floor.

"Yeah, baby, I'm in here."

I followed his voice to the kitchen. He interrupted his breakfast to give me a hug.

"You hungry? Want something?" he asked.

"No, I'm fine, Dad. Had something before I left."

"How'd it go then? I put it on the TV for a bit but I didn't see you."

"Really?"

I smirked to myself. It instantly came to mind the times the guys had said their parents had said the same things to them, whenever they'd been to a televised gig. The guys had been to a few festivals: T in the Park, the V Festival. Not like me; this was my first one. Parents though, they do make you laugh, some of the things they come out with. I grabbed my stuff and headed for the staircase.

"Gabriel called yesterday."

I was a little shocked by his words at first. Gabriel here? What was he doing here?

"Gabriel was here?" I asked as I returned to the kitchen.

"Yes. Yesterday morning I think. Yeah, that's right. You two fallen out or something?" he asked, looking slightly curious.

"No. Why do you ask?"

"I don't know, there was something uncomfortable about him. He didn't seem very talkative, not that he talks much anyway, but I don't know, less than normal I guess. Anyway, he didn't stay long. I said I would let you know he'd called but he told me not to worry, which is why I thought you two had had a falling out. Let's just say his behaviour seemed a little odd, that's all," he explained, concentrating on his half-eaten breakfast.

I could see he wasn't totally satisfied, watching him trying to work it out. I didn't comment further. I was a little confused.

"OK, Dad, I'll see you later."

Every step I took on the stairs now was accompanied by my thoughts as I tried to understand it. He had been here, came looking for me, but why after all this time? It didn't make any sense at all.

26

New Beginnings

I'd planned to have a quick nap to revive myself from the journey home but the constant thoughts that Dad had put in my head weren't helping. What was Gabriel doing here? He hadn't tried contacting me on my cell. I quickly retrieved it from my bag and searched the missed calls, in case I had missed him somehow. But as I suspected, there was nothing. Without giving it a thought I thumbed his contact number.

I stared at his name, as I felt a wave of emotion take over me. It had been such a long time. My stomach was doing somersaults, my head was all light and airy again. I desperately wanted to ring the number but my nerves wouldn't allow me. Yet I needed to know what he wanted. Why had he come back? And I needed to know now.

"Dad, I need to borrow the car." I said in a rushed voice, flying down the stairs, stumbling on the bottom step, regaining my composure before anyone could have seen.

"Yeah, course you can. You going to see the boys again?" he asked.

"No, no. I'm going up to see Gabriel," I said as I grabbed the keys from the hook.

"Oh, OK. Well, see you later." I caught his words as I was pulling the front door behind me.

"Yeah, laters."

I neared his house. The drive up had been a bit of a blur, my head full of questions and reasoning, all with a nervousness flowing through me. The thought of seeing him again was overwhelmingly intoxicating. I could feel my body going cold. Prickly bumps emerged on my arms, and yet the sun was still warm. I reached the end of his driveway in no time and spied his car parked there.

My body was a bumbling mess; no control, my legs weak standing in the porch, waiting for some reaction to the ringing of the bell. I tried again, but again no answer. I sensed my body had relaxed slightly. Strange his car was here. I was distracted by faint voices from around the side of the house, and I went to investigate. I could make out a man and a woman talking to each other but about what, I had no idea. And then I heard laughter as I walked towards them. The voices became stronger as I neared the end of the clearing. Gabriel was here! An automatic smile struck my face as I heard his voice. The female voice I did not know. There was a moment of silence as I turned the corner. I think my excitement at seeing him was at fever pitch. However, the scene that met me wasn't what I had expected. I stopped in my tracks, a little taken back by what was in front of me.

Gabriel and some woman stood together in the distance. He was facing me, her back was towards me, but he was unaware of me even being there. His arms were embracing her. I stood there stunned, unable to move, think, or feel anything about the scene facing me. The excitement instantly left me, replaced by nothing at first and then confusion, as I watched Gabriel kiss her. My eyes welling up as confusion turned to hurt and hurt turning to sadness. I did nothing, could do nothing, except stare, tears spilling down my cheeks as the details consumed me. I didn't make a sound or move a muscle but somehow I attracted Gabriel's attention. He had seen me. And without a moment's hesitation he released the woman from his grasp and headed towards me. I didn't want this now. I didn't want him anywhere near me. The pain in my chest was at crushing point, tears streaming uncontrollably now down my face. No way did I want him seeing me this way, my vulnerability exposed. I just wanted to get the hell out of there.

"Helena?" I heard him call from behind me as I sprinted towards the car. "Helena! Please wait."

I didn't want to talk to him. I had no interest in listening to his excuses. I could feel my breathing getting heavier, my heart beating, sounding in my ear. The engine quickly turned over as I selected the right gear. My hand hovered over the handbrake, Gabriel persistently trying to get my response.

"Helena, please stop! Just let me explain. It's not what you..."

"Think. Is that what you were going to say? Of course you'd say that. You must think I'm stupid. I just witnessed it with my own eyes. Of course it's what I think!" My voice sounded impatient. I tried to keep it together but I'm sure my annoyance showed.

In the heat of the moment I felt Gabriel grab my arm. The gesture surprisingly made me relax. I wasn't sure whether or not he'd sensed it but I wasn't about to give him the satisfaction in this situation.

"Hels! Please, just let me explain. It really isn't what you saw," he said in a very low, velvety voice.

My head was saying, tell him to get lost, but my heart had accepted his explanation and I was once again putty in his hands. However, the image of what I had just witnessed replayed vividly in my mind and my head got the better of me. I pulled my arm away from his grasp.

"Gabriel! I'm really not interested in your lame excuses. I only came here to see why you had returned. I thought perhaps you had changed your..." I shook my head. What was I doing? Just go home. He's clearly moved on. "Look it doesn't matter," I said, agitated, as I selected the correct gear and pulled away.

I watched Gabriel, looking deflated behind me, as I glanced in the rear view mirror. A moment of guilt struck me but was quickly replaced by a mixture of sadness, anger and embarrassment at the image that was etched in my mind. I didn't know what to do with all of these feelings; they were all muddled. I was shaking, so much so that I had to pull over to the side of the road. Tears had already welled in my eyes. It didn't take much for my self-control to fail, and they spilled out in an uncontrollable sobbing session.

The rest of the journey home was done in a daze. My mind constantly returned to the image of Gabriel and that woman all over each other. Each time brought me to my knees emotionally. The pain in my chest from the constant tears was physically unbearable, pounding so heavily.

Dad was surprised I was back so soon but I made out that I hadn't seen Gabriel. I wasn't in the mood to tell the truth, not now anyway, and he didn't pursue the matter. I was just glad he was otherwise occupied with sorting out his fishing box, which gave him less chance to notice my face, red with my persistent crying.

I could hear my cell ringing again as I made my way upstairs. I didn't answer it. I knew it was him. It hadn't stopped ringing since I left his house. A part of me was anxious to answer it and hear his voice again. I wish Mum was here; she'd know what to do! She always had a sensible way of dealing with things. She had a way of calming things down and looking at them logically, especially about emotional stuff. My mother and father were a great match in my opinion! Mum had the attributes of realism and calm, and Dad energy and fun-loving. I could talk to Dad about this stuff too but I tended not to. It was girlie stuff. I really wanted a woman's thoughts on it but I wasn't going to get that. So

I needed to sort this myself! Eventually I gave in to my intuition. I looked at my cell. I had three missed calls, which meant three voice messages.

They were all from Gabriel, apologising, trying to give me an explanation for what I had witnessed. His voice had a pleading ring to it, trying to reassure me that what I'd witnessed was not how it seemed. By the sound of it, he desperately wanted me to know the truth, to give him a chance to explain. And most of my inner feelings were saying, why not hear him out? He deserves that at least. I played with the necklace around my neck that my mother had given me as a child, as I contemplated my decision. It reminded me of the time when I stayed at his house and he asked me about it. I was intrigued at how interested he was in it. I never knew why. I twiddled it between my fingers, my thoughts turning to my mother and how she would have guided me if she had been here, and I was pretty sure that she would have encouraged me to listen to Gabriel, to give him a chance to explain. Knowing that made it feel right. I didn't need to think about this any more. No more torturing myself over whether I should or shouldn't. It needed sorting out. I grabbed my jacket from the chair.

It wasn't long before I was parked again on Gabriel's driveway. My heart pounded all the while as I walked towards the front door. I felt nervous. I wasn't sure why but it really was an uncomfortable feeling. It probably had something to do with my last encounter here not being what I expected. I'd gone from being on a high to ground zero in a split second. I hated thinking about that now. I needed to focus and not be left on this porch too long, reliving the past. Almost as if he had read my mind, the door opened. His expression was one of surprise. Gabriel's hand movements and facial features seemed uneasy as he gestured for me to follow. I made a point of scanning the rooms as we passed through to the lounge. I don't know what I was expecting to see. If she was here, I guess, the other woman I mean, but no doubt she'd be upstairs. But as I thought about it I realised I had come up here unexpectedly so there would have been no time for him to hide her from me.

I could feel the tension between us spilling out in awkwardness. Both of us attempted to maintain the usual pleasantries but were boiling underneath with questions and excuses. The conversation was kept to a minimum at first. Gabriel, I presumed, was waiting to gauge my emotions before he committed himself. But actually I was feeling very relaxed, considering how I felt a few hours before. I was inwardly pleased to be here again, in his company, something that I knew I had missed for so long. When I was around him, everything seemed less difficult, complicated. He had that way about him that just mellowed you out. But for all of that, there were things I needed to know from him.

"So! You said it wasn't what I thought. Well, how is it then?" I asked him.

Gabriel got settled opposite me. He was looking a little uncomfortable but I guess that was to be expected after our last encounter.

"Yes, that's right."

I could see he was uneasy about the whole thing. He almost looked as though he was somewhere else, maybe upstairs with her.

"Gabriel? The woman?"

"Yes, of course. The woman you saw me with was in actual fact my cousin Sarah. She has been staying here a while."

I was shocked. I hadn't bargained on that. I didn't even know he had one.

"It was her who encouraged me to finally come to see you at your father's."

I moved forward in my seat. I was intrigued and wanted to know more.

"Hang on a minute. Your cousin? You've never mentioned her before. Why didn't you say that?" I still wasn't so convinced.

He shot me a questioning look.

"Perhaps I didn't get the chance," he replied softly.

"OK, so I deserve that. But you were kissing her. I saw you and it didn't look like a family kind of kiss. It sure looked more than that from where I was standing."

He too moved forward in his seat.

"Hels, you're right. I was kissing Sarah as you saw but what you didn't know was that we were acting out. She wanted to know what it was like."

"And did she find out?" Instantly feeling the hurt within me, I shot back my answer in what probably came across as a jealous remark.

His facial expression showed his understanding of my comment.

"Helena! I didn't explain myself properly. What I meant to say was that she has never experienced the emotions of others before. She was curious. She wanted to know how that would feel."

My jealous reaction turned to confusion. "So you mean to tell me she's never been kissed before. Come on, do you think I'm stupid? From what I could see, she's a pretty woman. She's probably had loads of guys falling over her. Look, if you and her have something going on, just say so. I won't get in the way." Saying it was one thing but meaning it was another. I really wasn't sure what was going on here. Was he making this up?

"No! Look, I'm really not doing this right. Sarah! My cousin. Well, it's true she's never been kissed but that probably has something to do with the fact that she too has been gifted."

I guess my expression showed the difficulty I was having with this.

"An angel!" Gabriel had guessed my thoughts.

"But I could see her," I said, still puzzled.

"Yes, I know. She thought that was strange too. She's never found anyone who has been able to see her before, hence she has never experienced human emotions before. I was just trying to demonstrate a little of what we once shared, that's all."

I felt an instant warmth knowing that he still regarded our relationship as something so special that he wanted to share it with others. It also made me feel a little foolish.

"Oh! I see. So are you two close then? It's just you've never mentioned her before," I asked inquisitively.

"You know, since I found out who I am, I know more about my family ties. Before, I didn't even know I had a cousin but so much more has been explained to me. Sarah says I'm so lucky to have experienced different emotions. She thinks it's because I was given the opportunity to have human feelings before knowing who I was. You see, she has always known who she was, right from the beginning, but with my mother dying when I was so young, it was felt that it was better to wait to tell me until I was old enough to take it on board."

I had to take a minute to take in all that Gabriel had said. "So, you haven't told me why you're back here."

"Hmm, well, to be honest it took me a long time to pluck up the courage to come and see you. Sarah piled on the pressure though. She said I was a fool to let go of something so precious." He smiled in my direction. "She was right! I was stupid. Stubborn. I didn't realise how lucky I was. My mother said there are very few of us who have the chance to have this kind of bond with a human. However, I hadn't told her the real details behind us. I listened to a story she had told about herself, which I had no idea of before. She too had a special relationship with a human and she explained this as the most special moment in her life, at a time when things weren't great for her.

"I didn't get her to elaborate on the details. She seemed to be so sad at the mere remembrance of it. So I guess it runs in the family, this link with human life. But I agree with her, it is the most special thing we angels get the privilege to encounter."

He looked so humbled, explaining how much our past closeness had meant to him.

"So what are you saying then?" I asked.

I watched as he twiddled his fingers, his head hung down, as if to watch their movements, but I sensed that his mind really wasn't on what was in front of his eyes, rather the various thoughts going through his mind right then.

There was something really quite attractive about his posture; it showed a vulnerability, an insecurity, about his feelings, like he wasn't taking anything for granted.

"Helena, can you not tell what I'm trying to say? This is not the easiest of things to say for someone like me."

He looked deep in thought but not at ease with himself.

"Gabriel! I think I know what you are trying to say but I need you to say it. I need to know you're sure about this. And hey! If it makes any difference, angel or human, men fill themselves with dread at the mere thought of doing this speech, so give yourself a break."

His head was still hung in his lap. I caught the slightest of smiles as it flashed across his face.

"Really! So I'm not so different then?" he said, as he rose to his feet.

I joined him.

"No, you're not, not at all," I whispered, as I grabbed at his hand hanging by his side. "Gabriel, I don't know how this is going to pan out. Nobody does. You just have to enjoy the ride for as long as it lasts. And yes, it may not last forever but what's the alternative? You tried that already and I guess from your return that it didn't go so well?"

I took a moment to reflect on those weeks after Gabriel decided that he could not keep our relationship, that he thought distance would release him from all those feelings we had shared. The emptiness his decision had caused in my very existence had left a definite scar. I had found it so hard to pick up the pieces of the life I once had before him.

"I'm so sorry, Helena. I didn't know what else to do. I never meant to cause you so much pain. It was the last thing I wanted to do," he said.

We were once again in tune with one another. He'd heard my thoughts, just like before.

"But you're right. No one can guarantee anything, but it took me so long to realise that and in the meantime I managed to hurt the most important person to me." He shot me a knowing look. "I really do hope you can learn to forgive me, Helena."

He looked as though he was really waiting for my answer, not just giving me a throwaway line of sorts. I didn't have to think about my answer. I knew from the moment I left home that forgiveness was not a problem. I knew that Gabriel would come right, that all that had gone before, the girl in his arms, that there was bound to be a logical reason for it all.

"OK, but if I do forgive you, what's in it for me?" I asked, thinking a comical tone would fit in quite nicely now, lighten the mood a bit.

He looked a little mystified, as if to say, "I wasn't expecting that." A few moments of silence passed before he delivered his answer.

"Me! If that's OK with you?" he said.

It was my turn to feel the effects of an unexpected answer.

"Wow! Wasn't expecting that. Hoping yes, expecting no."

"So what were you expecting?" he asked.

"I don't know. This I hoped for but didn't think you were ready for it," I said.

"Yeah, you're right. I was scared, I guess. I didn't think I could give you all you needed, the things you would want over a period of time. I didn't know how I would fit in. I was scared you would want more than I could give you."

I could feel the sincerity of his words, the depth with which they were spoken. And although I didn't understand that at the time, I could see that now. I think for the first time my senses were really open. I could feel how anxious Gabriel was to make me happy… the apprehension over the unknown, the fear of failure and the pain of loss.

All the things he was so desperate to taste with me that his need outweighed the reasons not to do so.

Both my hands were in his now, still by our sides. I could feel the strength of the moment, the intensity of the feelings we shared for one another, as if they had never been away.

We stared at each for what seemed a lifetime, caught in the wonder of this moment. Yes, we'd been here before but it was different this time, as though we'd woken up from a dream and this all made sense. It was right, real and meant to be. He bent his head to rest on my forehead. I really had missed this whole thing.

"Well, what do you think?" he whispered so sweetly.

I could feel his hot breath on my skin, sending me into submission. My eyes were closed but felt open. I drifted through white light at first, and then shades of light blue and white. The sun shone on my face as I felt its glow. There was no harshness to the heat but pleasant warmth. I could hear the sounds of waves washing against a shoreline. The smell of sea salt as it lay beneath me. The warmth of the sand as I dug my toes into it. I flinched at the tug at my hand, as I realised Gabriel was still holding it. His warm, friendly smile beamed down at me, making me feel safe and secure. My eyes were drawn to the source of the noises around me. The beach was packed with people everywhere, enjoying the day. Some were families, kids playing in the sand, grandparents and couples all enjoying the moment. And by each group stood a person dressed not for the weather at all but for something more formal.

I recognised the attire from some place before. It seemed familiar but I couldn't put my finger on it. They were everywhere. They either stood or knelt beside the groups of people. As I watched, there were no words spoken to them or even by them. They just smiled at what they could see, as if they were just spectators.

"This is who I am, Helena. All that I am, I give to you, if this is what you want." I heard these words and turned to look at Gabriel by my side. The question needed no answer; surely he knew this. I was his before I or he even knew it.

"Yes," I whispered, as I nestled into his chest, his head resting on mine.

The drifting feeling stopped, and I opened my eyes to see that nothing had changed. I was still in the same position as before. Gabriel lifted his head from mine, as he looked down at me and smiled.

"Helena, I am now bound to you. I am your heavenly host, your companion, here on earth for as long as you need me or until our worlds meet," he whispered.

"Gabriel?"

"Yes?" he said, as his fingers traced my face and then down my neck. He studied me tenderly.

My heart was pounding with the intensity of the moment. I wanted him more than anything I knew before.

"Kiss me!" I whispered.

He smiled, as he gently guided his fingers across my mouth, as if to caress them. My lips parted from his touch. The warmth of his mouth on mine was intoxicating and I felt utterly powerless in this hypnotic, dream state in which I now found myself. I was riveted to his very soul.

27

My Host

The drive home was far too fast for my liking. Gabriel had insisted on taking Dad's car back. He was the practical one. I was still in a dream bubble from the day before.

I stayed over at his request. I hadn't wanted it any other way. There was so much to discuss, so much time to catch up on. Everything was proper though. I was in the guest room as before.

Gabriel wouldn't have had it any other way. I knew he had very old-fashioned values. He was old school; that's what I loved about him. He believed in really getting to know someone well. Not that he didn't have feelings just like any other man of his age, it was just that he had learned to control them. When we kissed I could feel the intense burning inside him, as I'm sure he sensed the same feelings in me, but he believed in getting it right. I smiled to myself as I remembered that topic of conversation during the night, along with many others. All the values he prided himself on really had more value now than he had anticipated, especially when relationships were a no-no for his kind.

"What?" he said, taking his eyes off the road to look at me.

"Nothing. I was just thinking how lucky I am to have found you," I said, as I grabbed his free hand, the one not holding the steering wheel.

"Oh! Well, on that score, I think I am the one that's lucky. Remember what my mother said?" he replied. "Helena, you are everything and more than I could have hoped to have in my life.

Believe me, I'm the lucky one!"

My hand was pulled towards his mouth, and his lips gently kissed the back of it. I smiled back in acknowledgement as we pulled into the driveway. As much as my emotions were saying, "To hell with work; I want to stay here with you," a small part of me knew I needed to keep some reality, some normality, in my life, and anyway my dad wouldn't be too happy if I jeopardised my job, my bit of independence.

Saying goodbye on the driveway, even for a short time, was so wonderfully hard. Each chance we had at kissing and even touching each other seemed more intense, heightened, unbearable, but in a great way.

Dad was in the doorway, aware I was watching him watching us. Strange that he did that. He hadn't done it before and looked very interested in something, long after I walked through the door.

"Hey, Dad, have the boys called at all?" I said, passing through and replacing the car keys on the hook.

"No." He remained on the doorstep, the front door wide open. He seemed preoccupied, as though he was looking for something.

"Was that Gabriel with you?"

"Yeah. He's gone home," I replied as I walked towards him.

I was getting really quite curious. He hadn't moved from the doorstep since I came in. Something had obviously got his attention. "He's coming back later," I said.

"Who's the woman with him?" he asked as I reached him at the door.

He hadn't changed his gaze. He was still looking intently in the direction Gabriel had just gone. I couldn't help but look myself. I couldn't see a thing. Quite frankly, I was a little confused at what had caught his attention and was still having that effect on him. But I was also aware he was asking a few questions in regards to

Gabriel. I wondered what he was getting at.

"What woman?" Even though I knew no one was there, I still looked.

"You didn't see her? She almost looked like your…"

He stopped.

I turned to face him. He had what could only be described as a look of shock, then bewilderment. He still seemed to be transfixed, focused on the route the now-departed Gabriel had walked. Really weird!

"Dad, there's no one there. Really, no one."

"You sure you didn't see her?" He was clearly not happy with the answer I gave.

"Dad, yeah I'm sure," I said, trying to divert his attention from what seemed like an obsession. I wanted to sort this out once and for all. He was clearly distressed about what he thought he saw and he wasn't letting it go. I was amazed by his determination to keep going with this. I grabbed my cell from the foot of the stairs, where I had flung it earlier. I made a quick call to ask Gabriel to clear up the mystery around this so-called woman. I was sure he'd be baffled by it as well, but surprisingly he wasn't. Moments later I returned to where Dad was still situated on the front step, showing no intention of moving anytime soon.

"Hey, Dad. I just spoke with Gabriel. You're right. There was a woman with him, although she wasn't there when he left me, so I don't know where she came from."

I realised I was babbling away to myself. "Helena?" said Dad, reminding me of the fact.

"Oh yeah. Well, it was his mother."

I briefly caught the quizzical look he gave me as I left him still standing there, confusion written all over his face. He said nothing as I took my leave and rushed upstairs, thinking no more of it.

Epilogue

Mike watched from the sidelines as his little girl shouted with earnestness and excitement at the momentum of the swing on which she sat, as it moved faster and higher into the daylight sky. He smiled as his daughter's change of expression moved from laughter to fear in a split second, whilst continuing to ask her mother to "Push higher, Mummy, higher."

His attention then turned to his wife, as she continued to grant her daughter's wishes. Still to this day he could not quite understand what this woman with such calibre would see in a man like him. She had saved him, found him at a time in his life when things could have been somewhat better. As he stared at her now, he still gasped at her beauty, a smile that characterized her, so warm and friendly. It reminded him of the time at the beach, here in Teignmouth, where he had met her so long ago. His own smile broadened as those early memories of her came to mind. She had not changed, not one little bit. She had somehow defied time, something he had not been so lucky in achieving himself. Even through Helena's difficult birth, she had gone through the experience gracefully and without complaint, instead viewing it as a privilege to have been given the opportunity in the first place. She was such a humble person.

Mike's focus came back to the scene in front of him. Helena's arm was wrapped tightly around her mother's neck as she was carried from one park apparatus to another. Her mother's arms were wrapped equally tightly around her daughter's back as she swung her around with such enthusiasm. Their energy focused on each other was an inspiration for him. Both laughed with delight, as she placed her daughter very gently on the deserted slide. It was truly mesmerising to watch.

His attention was diverted for a moment, as he felt the presence of a small hand take his own. A small boy with dark hair, about seven years of age, was standing at his side, looking up at him. The boy smiled broadly as Mike looked around for his mother. He returned the smile to keep the boy at ease, although the child seemed very relaxed in his company anyway. No words were spoken by either of them. The boy's little hand released his grip as he made his way towards the slide. Mike felt cold, almost shivery, as the boy walked away.

Mike was slightly apprehensive as he watched the scene unfold in front of his eyes, feeling like a mere spectator. He watched as his wife turned and walked towards this child. There were no words said, no sound, as if this scene was inside a bubble and he was watching from the outside. The comfortable feeling of watching his daughter and wife interact had now been replaced by a sense of uneasiness, but for what reason he did not know.

He watched carefully as his wife bent down to face the young boy. Mike took a look at his daughter as she continued to play, oblivious to her mother's distraction. His attention was swiftly called back to his wife. Still no words were exchanged between them, yet he had a feeling, watching this scene, that there was some familiarity between them, a connection of sorts, but it was hard to describe in detail. It made him feel kind of uneasy, as if they shared something, but only they knew what. He almost felt like he was an intruder, spying on them somehow. It really was a very uncomfortable feeling. His inner self was willing him to walk over to them, find out who this little guy was and get rid of this silly notion in his head.

He paused once more, distracted by his daughter's smile, her beautiful little fingers sifting through the sand as she sat in the pit, happily filling her trouser leg pockets with the soft sprinkly stuff that disappeared through her tiny fingers, unaware of anything else going on around her. For a brief moment that uneasiness was replaced by his delight in watching her. But the feeling returned as quickly as it was lost and his attention was diverted back again to his wife. The scene remained silent, still with that odd kind of bubble effect. Mike watched the boy lean forward towards his wife and wrap his tiny arms tightly around her neck. And still not one word was spoken between them. This strange scene unfolding in front of him made no sense at all. Once again his urge to investigate closer was replaced with caution, as if the task was inappropriate.

This was crazy! How was it that he was unable to get past being a spectator? Mike watched as his wife led this boy to the sandpit where his daughter still played, unaware of her daddy's discomfort. His need to move, to protect, be a part of his family and to be rid of this intrusion was heavily burdened by panic, an overbearing sense of fear, of not being worthy of her, of her love. He watched as his beloved family played at ease with this stranger, as if they belonged somehow. He studied her smile, as she watched over her flock protectively. Unable to move for fear of rejection, Mike's eyes pleaded for answers. But none were forthcoming. He continued to watch as the children played, happily sifting through the sand with their tiny fingers.

His eyes caught sight of a shiny object attached to something string-like wrapped around the boys fingers. The boy's eyes were full of fascination and wonder as he tried to unwrap the gold-coloured, sparkling rope from around his fingers. Mike caught a glimpse of a charm-like object dangling from it. Mike watched as the rays of sunlight made it glisten as it dangled there. There was something familiar about it. Even from here, he recognised this piece of jewellery. This had belonged to his daughter; he was sure of it. It was something her family had passed down to his wife. He watched as his wife carefully unwound the necklace from the boy's fingers and placed it around his neck. She kissed him gently on the forehead and turned her gaze solely on him. Still unable to protest for fear of rejection, Mike stood, confused by her action. Why had she given it to him? It wasn't his to have. It belonged to his little girl, who was unaware of her daddy's concerns. It just didn't make any sense! Why would she do that, giving it to a perfect stranger like that? The uneasiness remained with him. He was unable to fathom out what this all meant but knew that it did mean something. He searched himself for anything that would give rise to the answers he sought. His mind was heavy, burdened with the desire to know what was missing. He looked at the scene in front of him, as his beloved wife played with both children, unaware that he was even there. Surprised at how relaxed he now felt, he watched them intently, sensing his pride in what he cherished most, his beautiful family. His wife's smile met his, as though she had only now remembered he was there.

The energy within it was explosive and felt like he was summoned to her command. The children seemed to have felt the same. He studied them all in turn. His beautiful, sweet daughter with the lovely curls hanging around her face. His adorable wife, whom he cherished more than life itself, with her mesmerising porcelain face that won his heart from the start. And the boy.

Mike studied his face more deeply now. Somehow this child was familiar to him. His eyes had a deepness to them, like they weren't as young and unknowing as they should be.

Looking at the boy left Mike with a sense of confusion, as though there was something else, something he had not seen, something he had missed. Mike searched his inner self for anything that would give him the answers, searching his memories for anything that he had seen before, anything that perhaps had puzzled him before. And there it was! He had found it! Mike had been here before, searching for the same answer, puzzled by the resemblance.

"I know your face!"

And he did, he knew it all along!

Heavenly Host

The Concluding Journey

The Chains That Bind

Coming Soon